Charlie Milverton
and other
Sherlock Holmes
Stories

Charlotte Anne Walters

Paperback ISBN 978-1-78092-577-6
ePub ISBN 978-1-78092-578-3
PDF ISBN 978-1-78092-579-0

Published in the UK by MX Publishing
335 Princess Park Manor, Royal Drive, London, N11 3GX
www.mxpublishing.com

Cover design by www.staunch.com

Acknowledgements

Thank you to Sherlockology, The Undershaw Preservation Trust and MX Publishing for including Charlie Milverton in their publication Sherlock's Home, The Empty House.

Thank you to my husband Tim who patiently reads everything I write, also Janice and Louise who probably think I'm mad but support me anyway, and of course, the genius of Sir Arthur Conan Doyle.

Each story within this book has been inspired by an original Sherlock Holmes adventure created by Conan Doyle. I have simply updated them to 21st century scenarios and settings. Therefore, I cannot take full credit for all the plot twists, clues and concepts the stories contain, just their re-working into modern equivalents. The original stories I have used are; The Adventure of Charles Augustus Milverton, The Adventure of the Noble Bachelor, The Adventure of the Creeping Man, A Case of Identity and The Adventure of the Abbey Grange.

Contents

Charlie Milverton

Todd Carter rubbed his hands together excitedly then straightened the lapels of his designer suit.

"Well Mr Gareth Lestrade, on paper you stack up very nicely. Twenty years at Scotland Yard, senior police officer with all the relevant qualifications, but that's not enough. Think you've got what it takes to look after my girls? Prove it..."

He flashed a playful smile of whitened teeth then barked across to the burly, black-suited security guard standing by the door.

"Take him down Peterson," Todd commanded, adding a patronising wink. "This ain't Scotland Yard."

He shrugged off a pang of guilt; *well, if the agency does insist on sending these old men...*

Peterson rushed at Gareth, sixteen stone of muscle bearing down on him like a speeding train. This was shaping up to be the most surreal job interview imaginable.

Gareth had always been fairly adept at self-defence, but understood that to work in private security he needed to enhance his basic skills. Twelve months of unemployment had given him plenty of time.

He swiftly blocked his attacker; they grappled together before a final outburst of effort enabled him to send his opponent confidently to the floor. What he lacked in strength was compensated for in technique.

Todd was momentarily stunned by this unexpected outcome, although a face-full of Botox made it impossible to show it. He was becoming reluctantly impressed with this understated man who was clearly not a fame-hunter, kiss-and-tell merchant or someone who would have designs on his most precious possession, his girlfriend Della. *But could a forty-seven year old ex copper with a damaged reputation and no previous experience really look after a high-profile girl-band? Well, at least Della wouldn't want to sleep with him...*

....

Sherlock Holmes wasn't a sentimental man, but he did get used to certain people being in his world, like a favourite jacket or armchair. Detective Inspector Lestrade had been one of those people and now that he had gone, it was surprisingly unsettling.

So to find Lestrade back in his sitting room was comforting, a restoration of normality – except for Lestrade's expensive suit and LA tan.

"How is Doctor Watson?" Gareth asked, trying to ease in with general conversation.

"He has abandoned me for a wife."

"My wife abandoned me for a Chief Superintendent,"

"Not the same, her decision made sense."

"Thanks," replied Gareth sarcastically, greatly accustomed to Holmes' direct honesty.

"Smoke?"

"I don't, not now. I've just come back from LA, no one smokes – they all drink green-tea and have perfect teeth."

"You stopped off on the way back though, somewhere in Europe...Ibiza. All-inclusive 5 star hotel?"

This was what Holmes did, observed everything at lightning speed and made highly accurate inferences that would elude anyone of inferior brain.

"Don't look so surprised, you should know my methods by now. Your watch is two hours behind so not long-haul, and your boss owns a club in Ibiza I believe? You're wearing a hotel wrist-band so must have been all-inclusive and celebrities don't stay anywhere less than 5 star."

Gareth smiled, same old Holmes. They had known each other professionally for years but were not exactly friends. There were no normal conversations about family, football or last night's TV - such pleasantries would bore Holmes' hyperactive mind. But take him a problem, a perplexing murder, an odd series of apparently unconnected events, and he would come alive with furious energy.

"Why are you here Lestrade? You said you needed my help, so elaborate."

It had been a hectic twelve months, a real baptism-of-fire into the music business for an ex copper with no previous experience. Gareth felt as if he had travelled around the world and back again at least twice. He had seen more drugs, assaults and weapons than in the whole of his career on the force. A career that now lay in ruins.

"I've brought someone with me; they're waiting in the car. I wanted to see you first, make sure this would be something of interest to you. I know how scathing you can be towards a client if you find their situation disinteresting. And she's fragile, my job is to protect her – not expose her to your own peculiar brand of pleasantries."

"Della, I presume?"

"How do you know? There are three girls in the band."

"But Della has the highest profile, and it would take something serious to bring you to my door again."

"Holmes, I don't blame you for what happened..."

At which point the sitting room door opened and Della walked in. Dressed down in comfortable shoes, skinny jeans and a t-shirt she still looked strikingly attractive. A designer bag was slung over her shoulder and a huge pair of shades was pushed on top of her head, holding back a side-fringe of baby blonde hair.

"I'm sorry," she said, in a warm Northern accent, "I couldn't wait any longer. I'm going out of my mind Mr Holmes. The police aren't interested and Mr Lestrade said you could be trusted, that you help people. I really need help."

Della settled herself on the sofa next to Gareth, nervously rubbing together her hands.

"As you probably know, I'm a singer in a girl-band. I've worked so hard to get this far – I did my first talent contest aged five and was sending off demo tapes by the time I was fourteen. I'm twenty-nine now, but the record company tell everyone I'm twenty-four. Thank God for Botox or we'd never get away with it. Soon after getting signed to my label, I started dating my manager, Todd Carter. I was flattered, felt lucky he was interested in me. We've been together five years, we're even engaged. We're like one of those celebrity couples everyone loves to read about, Todd markets it for all it's worth – 'at home' shoots in magazines, pictures of us on yachts smiling like we're a devoted couple. Truth is, he's a control freak – even installed a tracker in my phone so that he always knows where I am. I can't breathe without his permission. He's got me on diets constantly, he's obsessed about me not looking my age – he's thirty-five and thinks it makes him seem younger if I look good. He's obsessed with his own looks too, had loads of cosmetic surgery. I won't say I'm afraid of him Mr Holmes but he's a powerful man, he made me and can break me just as quick. I don't have money of my own, he controls everything – I can't even buy a bagel without him knowing."

"I presume this is leading somewhere interesting?" Holmes asked impatiently.

"I'm seeing someone else Mr Holmes, someone who makes me happy. I'm not proud of it but in private Todd is cold, it's like he doesn't really want me but won't let anyone else have me. If he finds out, he'll destroy us both. I've been so careful, but something has happened – this evil, manipulating..."

Her voice choked as big fat tears tumbled from her wide, blue eyes. Gareth fished out a tissue and handed it to her. She composed herself enough to continue, holding Holmes' attention with her earnest expression.

"His name is Charlie Milverton. He preys on celebrities by getting his hands on anything which he can sell to the tabloids or spread on gossip websites. Then he makes contact and demands a fee in return for his silence. He's got so much dirt that everyone's afraid of him so his name never comes out – remember the MPs expenses scandal? The phone-tapping allegations? And then there was that young pop-star who killed himself after the papers published pictures of him taking drugs? All Milverton. Now he's set his sights on me and I don't know what to do. He has a security tape of me in a hotel lift kissing this other man. He's threatened to sell it unless I pay £200,000. I have nothing of my own; I can't pay Mr Holmes – not without Todd knowing. But if this comes out, my reputation will be ruined and that of the other person involved – who really doesn't deserve this. Please help me."

....

Doctor Watson enjoyed escaping normality to visit Holmes at 221b. But it was difficult now that he had commitments, tea on the table when he got home and Sunday lunch with the in-laws. However, he had received a summons from Holmes and obediently made his way round, while his wife was at Pilates. As instructed, he brought with him all the information he had found from the internet about Charlie Milverton.

Holmes always acted impassively when Watson returned to his old rooms, but the doctor knew that his friend was secretively pleased to see him.

"Well," Watson exclaimed, throwing a pile of papers down on the coffee table, "I've been busy doing what you asked."

"Though not busy at work,"

"How do you know? I could have done all this at home."

"The paper quality is too good, you only buy cheap paper for home – that is clearly office stationary."

Watson was never particulary busy at work. He worked for a firm of solicitors who specialised in 'no-win-no-fee' compensations cases. His job was to assess a never-ending stream of wasters and sign the forms confirming they had whiplash, stress, a breakdown etc – even if they didn't.

"Charlie Milverton was a tabloid editor," Watson began, hoping to impress. "But he was ousted over drink problems.

He retreated into the shadows and used his vast media contacts for dark purposes. He is obsessed with celebrities. He's the go-to person if you have a tape, incriminating email, leaked document - he will purchase it from you then sell it on. He is believed to be behind several websites, mainly celebrity gossip but one which is more political and serious – though no one can prove it."

Watson sat back in his chair feeling hopeful that perhaps, for once, his friend might be impressed with his findings.

"A sterling effort Watson, though you have failed to discover the most important thing."

"Which is?" asked Watson, hurt but not altogether surprised.

"The legalities man! You work with lawyers - I need to know whether he's breaking any laws."

"I work *for* lawyers Holmes, there's a difference."

"Well, fortunately I anticipated your deficiencies and have consulted someone myself – a well-known celebrity lawyer who owed me a favour. Milverton acts fast, he makes sure the material is released before a Super Injunction can be sort – and the courts are becoming increasingly reluctant to protect self-serving celebrities. I have no choice but to negotiate with him on behalf of my client, he will be here within the hour. Do stay Watson, your wife intends to visit friends after Pilates – that's why she took the car and you came here in a cab. I can see the receipt sticking out of your trouser pocket, so useful for claiming expenses from those lawyers you slave for."

....

Charlie Milverton shuffled into the room. Overweight, ugly and short, clearly blackmail was his only way of getting close to the 'beautiful people' who had become his obsession.

Holmes tried to negotiate but the stubborn little man would not budge. A reduced fee or the promise of payments by instalments was not acceptable to him. Any attempt to play on his sympathies failed. Watson observed that Holmes became unusually flustered at Milverton's resolve, losing his usual cool in the face of such obstinacy. He finally rose from his seat and asked Milverton to leave, looking dejected and exhausted as the strange media-beast made his way to the door – smiling victoriously.

"Payment by Saturday Mr Holmes, or full disclosure will be my only option. Tell your client to pay up or face the consequences."

Holmes slammed the door behind him and sat back in his chair. Watson let the silence settle between them as Holmes' mind frantically worked over the problem. Eventually, knowing that his wife would be returning home soon, he stood to leave.

"My wife will flip out if I'm home late."

"Dreadful Americanism," grumbled Holmes. Then, suddenly, he rose and grabbed Watson by the shoulders.

"America! Brilliant Watson! Yet again you have proved to be invaluable without even realising. See yourself out…"

With that parting remark, Holmes grabbed his jacket and rushed from the room – full once again of that furious energy which usually spelt doom for his foes.

……..

Accustomed as he was to his friend's rapid concluding of cases, even Watson was shocked when he turned on the TV news Friday morning and saw that Milverton had been arrested. The ex-tabloid editor had been taken from his home during a dawn raid and was now in police custody. Watson didn't wait to hear the reporter's version of events and rushed straight to Baker Street. This was worth being late for work and risking the wrath of the ever-watchful lawyers.

"America Watson," Holmes proudly announced, looking like a man who had been up all night but was buzzing with adrenalin. "I owe you an apology, you're findings did prove crucial after all."

Watson was unaccustomed to apologies from Holmes. Usually his efforts were rewarded with criticism. After his first book had been published about their adventures together, Holmes was pretty scathing and described it as sensationalist, not focusing enough on his 'method'. But it was Gareth Lestrade who had suffered the most.

Holmes had always been happy for his name to be kept out of the papers and despite helping Scotland Yard to solve many high-profile cases, he never took the credit. As far as the public were concerned, Gareth and his colleagues had solved the cases themselves – their name and achievements lauded in the press. But when Watson's book was published, even though some years had passed, the public felt angry that the police had taken credit for the work of an amateur. Tax payer's money had been spent but it was an ordinary citizen who had saved the day. There was an outcry, an investigation, and ultimately Gareth paid the price. Though he hadn't been the only police officer to accept Holmes' help, he was made the scapegoat – which suited the Chief Superintendant very well considering his relationship with Gareth's wife.

There was a suspension, a disciplinary hearing, the option to remain at Scotland Yard if he took a demotion but the damage was already done. Gareth salvaged whatever dignity he had left and resigned – shortly followed by the departure of his wife and a very costly divorce.

"I looked through your notes," Holmes announced. "You mentioned that Milverton was behind a political website, www.ileaks.com. Interesting stuff - particularly the allegations of corruption in the White House. This was exactly what I needed. You see, though Milverton's activities are not illegal here, the Americans take a dimmer view of such matters – especially if there is any suspicion of risk to national security. I just needed to find something which would be a breach of American law and then I could by-pass our own legal system. The US has powers under the Extradition Act of 2003 to extradite UK citizens for offenses committed against US law or security, even though the offense may have been committed here. Only a low level of proof is required, suspicion is enough for the US to demand that the person is taken into custody prior to extradition being granted. Well, Interpol were very interested when I gave them the findings of my little investigation into ileaks. Our friend Milverton has been using information acquired from a White House mole and by publishing it he has stirred up the wrath of our American cousins. The police have impounded his computers, documents and storage devices, even his phone. But fortunately, thanks to a few remaining contacts on the force, I did manage to salvage some salacious bits and pieces – including..."

He held up a memory stick in front of Watson's startled face.

"Is that Della's lift footage?"

"I can't guarantee that there haven't been copies made, but no editor will now touch anything from such a risky source."

....

Several weeks passed before Watson was able to sneak away from domestic bliss and visit his friend again. Once installed in his usual chair, Watson pushed for more information about Della and what the future now held for her. If he was going to write this up for his next book, he needed a better ending.

"This solves her immediate problem but she's still stuck with that awful man controlling her life," Watson commented.

"Not so. An opportunity is coming for her to walk away with the public firmly on her side. She wasn't the only person to be caught on camera with someone else that night."

"Carter was with someone too? How do you know?"

"I managed to find the source of the tape, a member of staff at the hotel. Fortunately, after a quick check with the Home Office, I confirmed that he was working here illegally. The threat of deportation was enough to ensure his compliance and I got him to search through the security footage from the corridor outside Carter's room. Carter brought someone back and they most helpfully began their 'enjoyment' outside in the corridor. The images are now with every tabloid editor, a little gift from me. Your Sunday paper should make interesting reading."

"That's brilliant. But, I have to admit being surprised that you would go to so much effort to help Della – problems matter to you, not particularly the people involved. You'd already stopped Milverton, why go the extra mile?"

"To help a good man get his woman, I suppose. Perhaps I felt I owed it to him. And I had nothing better to do."

"You mean the man in the lift with her? So you did watch it? Who was he? Celebrity-type I suppose."

"See for yourself..."

Holmes pushed the memory stick into his laptop and opened up the file. Watson watched the screen intently. There, he saw Della walk into the lift followed by her security manager. Once the doors closed, she flicked a switch which caused the lift to shudder and stop. She laid a hand on Lestrade's arm and pulled him close as he kissed her.

"Oh my God," Watson exclaimed, watching in disbelief. "Did you know?"

"Of course I knew."

"Did he tell you?"

"No."

"Then how...?"

"It was the socks. They were both wearing identical socks when I met Della, clearly men's. Pop-stars don't generally share socks with their security staff. They were wearing the same expensive make of watch too and the insignia on her bag was the same as on his belt. Matching socks, matching brands, even you could have worked it out Watson. Besides, if Carter really was watching her that closely, the lover had to be someone around her every day who he didn't suspect – a middle-aged security manager matches that profile rather well don't you think?"

"So the good guy takes the girl," smiled Watson, "with a little help from his friends..."

The Premier Bachelor

"It's no good John," uttered the seasoned literary agent, his weary expression betraying his general lack of interest in Watson's proposition. "I can't get you another book deal when sales of the first one are stagnating. You're competing in a tough market, up against celebrities like Kathy Rice. I've just negotiated a three-book-deal for her. An advance as big as her breasts."

"But she can't write for toffee!"

"No, but her ghost-writer can. And she's got a 30HH chest, that's a lot of boob John. Glamour models sell books. Especially ones with their own reality TV show who are about to marry a premiership footballer. An unknown doctor doesn't quite attract that level of attention, I'm afraid. In fact, you and your book haven't attracted much attention at all. Except for that fuss about Scotland Yard but everyone's forgotten it now. I have to be honest; I'm not sure how much longer I can go on representing you. Perhaps you should just stick to the day job Doctor Watson, eh?"

....

It wasn't supposed to be like this, Watson thought as he walked home from his agent's office. It had been five years since he left the army due to injury and found himself alone in one of the world's most exciting cities. He had felt an exhilarating sense of freedom, of possibilities to be explored. He would get work, save enough to pay for his GP exams and start working for a good practice, get a lovely house, marry, have children. Between patients he would write that bestseller he'd always dreamt of producing. A lucrative publishing contract would follow and he could retire early from medicine, spend his days writing books and being the toast of the literary world. Little did Watson realise that his dreams would be hampered by a lack of fake boobs. Or not raising the money for his GP exams and having to work in 'no-win-no-fee' hell.

His journey into the literary world had been fraught with difficulties from the start. The initial elation over having his first book published quickly subsided when faced with Holmes' scathing criticism of his accounts detailing their adventures since becoming flatmates – and the consequences for poor Gareth Lestrade. Knowing he had ended someone's career by trying to kick-start his own was awful. Then, despite a flurry of initial sales, the public didn't really share Watson's fascination with his friend's remarkable mind and the profession it had enabled him to carve out for himself. Consigned to bargain-bins while books by celebrity authors took pride-of-place in the bookstores, chances of improving sales were unlikely. Now he was faced with losing his agent and his literary dream was fading fast.

He could try and publish the story of how Holmes helped pop star Della Breton escape the clutches of a master blackmailer and hide her affair with her security manager. His agent's eyes would light up at the mere mention of a celebrity, but he couldn't do that to Lestrade, not again. He'd sacrificed most of his morals working for the lawyers; he was keen to hang on to the few he had left. At least he still had his friendship with Holmes. And though they were no longer flatmates due to Watson's marriage, they still shared the occasional adventure. This provided a welcome distraction for Watson from the humdrum monotony of his everyday life - but his wife didn't approve. She thought he was a bit of a dreamer, 'playing at being a detective's assistant', 'playing at being a writer' – too old to be playing at anything. She wanted him to grow up, settle down and accept that life is boring, that's the reality for most people. But he still made his way around to 221b Baker Street whenever he had chance.

....

Watson was surprised when his phone rang and he saw his agent's name come up as the caller. He hurriedly finished his consultation with a young man claiming to have whiplash from a car accident so minor that the person who rear-ended him caused nothing more than a cracked number-plate. The situation had 'crash-for-cash' written all over it but Watson hastily signed the forms and ushered the 'victim' out of his office so that he could return the call. He felt a knot of stress tightening in his stomach knowing that this could be the final phone call, the one in which he got officially dropped by his agent - the only agent who had been willing to take him on out of the fifty he had applied to. Instead, Larry Defonte's booming, self-important voice was full of warmth and friendly intonations as soon as he answered.

"Oh John, so good of you to call me back. Many apologies for calling you like this in the middle of the working day. Truth is, I need your help. Don't want to involve the police and need to keep it out of the press. A very lucrative three-book-deal now hangs in the balance. Oh dear, I'm fraught with worry. It's Kathy Rice, she with the 30HH you-know-whats. She's disappeared; no-one has seen her since Saturday afternoon – walked down the aisle happy-as-you-like, said 'I do' then pissed off before the reception and vanished into thin air! Thin air John!" he bellowed, his pitch increasing rapidly along with his anxiety. "I was hoping that your Mr Holmes might be willing to help me, hoping perhaps that you would consider introducing us and urge him to take the case."

Watson was rather ashamed that his initial thought was not for the safety of the missing glamour girl, but rather that helping his agent to find her and avert the catastrophe of losing a valuable book-deal, might save his own literary prospects. *"I really am running out of morals,"* he sighed, before putting on his most soothing voice and offering to call Holmes immediately to secure his assistance and pushing himself ever further down the slippery slope towards moral bankruptcy.

Sherlock Holmes, on the other hand, was very much a man of scruples and professional integrity. This was something which the handsome young footballer found very frustrating when they eventually came face-to-face at 221b that evening. Initially reluctant to take this case and distinctly unimpressed by the celebrity status of those involved, Holmes had taken some serious persuading from Watson. He only agreed to a meeting on the condition that he wouldn't take things any further unless the case presented factors which were of genuine interest to him.

Rich, good looking, arrogant and rather stupid, footballer Jimmy Jones was of no interest to Holmes whatsoever. Something which he did little to hide.

They all sat in the untidy living room at 221b – Watson, Larry Defonte, Jimmy Jones and his agent, the wealthy and powerful Rico Tandy. Holmes was standing, his tall and lean frame leaning casually against the mantelshelf.

"Well," said Holmes with a sarcastic smile, "I'm a busy man gentlemen and I'm afraid I can be of no further use to you. So, I must ask you to leave. I was listening to a scintillating piece of choral music when you arrived and I'm keen to get back to it. So, if you'll excuse me..."

"Mr Holmes," said Rico, sitting forward in his seat. "I don't think you understand the delicacy of the situation or the financial rewards we are willing to offer in return for a resolution. My client is one of the highest paid players in the premier league and a powerful figure in the world of celebrity. I doubt you have had such an opportunity presented to you before," he asserted, looking distastefully at the shabby surroundings.

"That would rather depend on whether you regard the head of one of Europe's oldest royal families as a celebrity. He was the last person to sit in that chair Mr Rico. And, I must add, he fitted it rather more neatly than you do."

Just as the bulky football agent was about to heave himself out of the seat in protest, Watson interjected.

"Holmes, why do you feel you can't help?"

"Because I cannot help anyone who doesn't tell me the truth."

"My client has taken a great risk in coming here and he has told no lies Mr Holmes," Rico insisted.

"Then where is his wedding ring? And why not go to the police?" Holmes turned to the nervous young player, "Mr Jones, you claim to love Miss Rice but here you are only 48 hours after she slipped a ring on your figure and you are sitting here without it – without any indentation around the base of your finger to suggest you wore it beyond the ceremony. And upon realising that your new wife has disappeared, your first thought is not to call the police but to summon your agent. You then continue to keep the disappearance a secret to protect your reputation – something which clearly means more to you than she does – and consult an unofficial person like me instead. Presumably because you think you can buy not only my services but also my silence. Well, you'll be disappointed to know that I cannot be bought, do not find your case interesting and will not deal with anyone who does not tell the truth." At which point he flamboyantly flicked a switch on his sound-system and the room was flooded with the celestial sound of choral music, which he proceeded to turn up to almost deafening levels. Watson could sense his literary career get up and leave the room.

Holmes didn't turn down the music until the dejected trio had closed the door behind them as they left.

"Don't look so worried," he said calmly, smiling at Watson's anxious face. "They'll be back."

"Defonte is about to drop me you know."

"I know,"

"How could you possibly know that?"

"Because of your wristwatch."

"Right, this is another one of those where you have to talk me through it. I will look astounded, you will look like a smug know-it-all and I will make a mental note to write it down for my next book. A book which no one will want to publish now that I'm about to lose my agent simply because you are too high-and-mighty to turn that massive intellect of yours to finding a glamour model who doesn't deserve a book deal anyway. She doesn't even write them herself. It's a joke."

"Simple. I knew you had a meeting with your agent on Friday to discuss a new book. Whenever things go really well for you professionally, you always celebrate by rushing out and treating yourself to a new watch. You bought that one when the dreadful lawyers gave you a pay-rise and haven't changed it since. The fact you are still wearing it suggests that a new book deal was not offered. As your first book isn't selling and a new deal is not on the cards, what possible incentive is there for Defonte to keep you on? You look astounded and I look smug, end of conversation."

He turned back up the choral music and closed his eyes in concentration. Watson sat in silence as he had done many times before.

....

Holmes was right, the trio did return much later that evening and Jimmy Jones confessed that he didn't really love Kathy Rice. It was a publicity stunt undertaken on the advice of both their agents to raise their profiles and give them maximum exposure. It had worked too – gossip magazines had lapped up the story of a promiscuous bad-boy footballer falling in love with the nation's favourite glamour girl who had been lucky in everything except love. They had sold the photographic rights of the wedding to a glossy magazine for a six figure sum and the ceremony had been a showbiz wedding of epic proportions. All had gone well on the day, the bride had sashayed down the aisle in what could only be described as a big pink meringue, the celebrity guests cried in all the right places, both bride and groom said an enthusiastic "I do" and everyone headed for the reception. One minute Kathy was with Jimmy posing for photos in the grounds of the luxury hotel where the ceremony had taken place, the next she was gone and hadn't been seen since. She had slipped into the venue to answer her phone, which had been ringing loudly and annoying the photographer. She didn't return.

....

"How can one of the country's most recognisable women just disappear?" Watson asked Holmes as they walked around the sumptuous hotel the following day. "Especially as she was wearing a pink frock-horror that you couldn't miss even if you tried."

"The dress was quite something," the hotel manager added, nodding in agreement. He was showing them both around the scene of the wedding. They walked into a huge dining room which still had pink bows tied around the backs of the chairs and general wedding paraphernalia all around.

"Did the reception continue despite the absence of the bride?" Holmes asked, his keen eyes darting eagerly around the room.

"No. Guests were simply told that Miss Rice, or Mrs Jones as she is now, had been taken suddenly ill. They were informed that an ambulance was coming to take her to a private hospital and asked to leave. She had no family, only a best friend and two other bridesmaids who had to be told the truth. Myself and my head of security were also informed. We were already on high alert because of the press intrusion and that crazy woman who turned up just before the ceremony."

"What woman?" asked Holmes, suddenly pulled back from his observations by this unexpected remark.

"She accosted Mr Jones in the reception area, drunk and causing a scene. They were standing in front of my office so I heard bits of the conversation. She threatened to tell Miss Rice all about the affair, to reveal everything. She was very angry at him. I presume she was a lover he had jilted – it's no secret that Mr Jones has a rather colourful reputation when it comes to women. Typical footballer I suppose. Strange thing was, she didn't look like your typical WAG. Seemed quite plain to me."

"Perhaps that's why he ended the affair?" offered Watson, "She wasn't famous enough."

Holmes had turned away from them and was looking at the flower arrangements still standing in the middle of the tables. "Do you know who supplied the flowers?" he asked the manager.

"A local florist I think. They left a card with our wedding planner. I can find it for you."

"That would be most helpful, thank you. And I presume you have CCTV footage of the argument in reception with this 'plain' woman?"

"Yes Mr Holmes. I have been instructed by Mr Tandy to assist you in any way I can. You are welcome to view the tapes and anything else you might find helpful. We are as keen as anyone that the young woman is found safe and well."

"I would like to see the groom's suite please, the one he stayed in the night before the ceremony," Holmes asked, as the manager ushered them back into the palatial reception area.

"Of course Mr Holmes. Follow me."

The footballer's room was typically ostentatious, as you would expect from a hotel of this grandeur. No one stayed in it since Friday evening and Jones had left the hotel in such a hurry after his bride disappeared, that most of his things were still in the room. Holmes headed into the marble bathroom, picking up various toiletries and sniffing around in his usual way. He handed Watson a tube of cream from beside the mirror. Watson read the medical label stuck to the front.

"It's a steroid cream to treat psoriasis – the skin condition. Jimmy Jones must have psoriasis, and pretty bad judging by the size of this tube."

Holmes smiled a deep, satisfying smile and walked back into the bedroom. He proceeded to go through a pile of clothes tossed lazily onto a chair by the bed. He then had a quick hunt through the wardrobe.

"I've seen all I need to," he concluded. "Make your own way back Watson, I have a busy afternoon ahead of me and you won't be of any help. Meet me back at Baker Street, say 6pm?"

"Make it five Holmes, the wife will have dinner ready by six. You know how she gets about meal times."

Holmes rolled his eyes impatiently and agreed upon 5pm.

....

Watson arrived at 221b and was surprised upon entering the living room to see a beautiful bouquet of flowers upon the mantel shelf. Clearly Holmes had visited the florist. The rather less beautiful Detective Inspector Hopkins was settled on the sofa opposite Holmes. He nodded to Watson a casual greeting and then resumed the conversation the pair were having prior to his arrival.

"We found the dress floating down the Thames. It looked like a giant pink taffeta jelly-fish all torn into shreds. No blood on it but a struggle must have occurred for it to be ripped up like that. There are now growing concerns for her safety Mr Holmes. We have been informed by Rico Tandy that he has engaged you to investigate Miss Rice's disappearance so I've come to keep you informed. I know from past experience that it's better to work with you rather than against. Though I don't see what more you can really add. Our investigation has been quite thorough and I am already able to piece together roughly what happened. Though I still can't work out exactly where Miss Rice is."

"Then please, Inspector Hopkins, enlighten me," said Holmes, settling into his usual chair opposite the eager young investigator, a rueful smile playing at the corners of his thin lips. "I presume," he added, "that someone of your calibre would have noticed straight away the unusual table displays at the hotel? I'm sure that I wasted my time visiting the florist myself and should have known that a highly competent inspector such as yourself would already be following up that line of enquiry."

Hopkins looked bemused, just as Holmes knew he would. Toying with the official police was good sport.

"Well, in light of more important discoveries, I...erm...decided to concentrate our resources elsewhere."

"Then tell us please, we are all ears," said Holmes, flashing Watson a playful look which suggested that much sport was about to be had. Watson, as ever, was completely in the dark and would be late home for dinner again, one of his wife's many pet-hates.

"Straight away I knew that our priority should be to identify the woman Jones had been having an affair with – the one who turned up at the hotel threatening to reveal all. We checked the CCTV and thanks to my sergeant, an avid aficionado on all sporting matters, he identified her straight away as the wife of non-other but Jones' agent – Rico Tandy. So, already we have a picture emerging," asserted Hopkins, who by now had stood and was starting to pace with his hands clasped behind his back.

"It is clear that Mrs Tandy has been having a relationship with her husband's star player. But Jones ended the relationship in favour of Miss Rice – a far more suitable celebrity match and one which would not cost him his agent, the very man who had orchestrated his success from a non-league side to top-flight international football. Jilted and angry, she got drunk and turned up on his wedding day to cause trouble. He sent her packing and she has taken her revenge by doing something to Miss Rice."

"And have you arrested her?"

"We've brought her in for questioning but she's saying nothing. Just keeps crying and giving 'no comment'. She's acting shifty though, clearly hiding something."

"Do have any actual evidence to link her to the disappearance of Kathy Rice?"

Hopkins fidgeted nervously, "Well no, not forensically speaking. It's all just circumstantial at the moment but it's pretty clear what went on. And if she's innocent, why doesn't she just say so instead of refusing to answer our questions? I've seen the CCTV of her altercation with Jones, it's pretty heated and she's highly agitated. Just a shame we can't hear what they are saying. She's drunk, swaying like a ship at sea, and he clearly just wants to get rid of her. She's furious, waving her arms at him, pushing him before she finally storms off. My theory is that she then tracks down his new bride and takes her revenge. But you're right Holmes, I need evidence. I can't hold her much longer without it. Did you find anything at the hotel?"

"I found plenty at the hotel," Holmes replied, lazily picking up some sheet music from a messy pile of papers scattered on the floor. He started idly fingering through it while Watson and Hopkins sat awkwardly in the silence, awaiting his elaboration. It never came.

Eventually, Hopkins let out a long, exasperated sigh.

"Clearly you are keeping your cards close to your chest, but I hope this means that you are still on board with the investigation. I have to say Holmes, I'm more than a little disappointed by your lack of input at this stage. I do hope you aren't losing your touch. After all, the safety of a young woman may be at risk."

"Thank you for your information about Mrs Tandy, Hopkins. It has somewhat confirmed a little theory of my own. See yourself out, would you?" added Holmes briskly, despatching the young inspector with a dismissive wave of his hand.

....

"You have a theory then?" Watson asked after seeing Hopkins to the door. His own manners often stepped in to make up for Holmes' lack of social etiquette. Holmes lifted his violin and started scratching away, the sheet music poised on his knee. "If you have any ideas Holmes, shouldn't you be sharing them with the police? I mean, Hopkins is right, this girl could be in danger."

Holmes lowered his violin briefly.

"She's not in danger. I know where she is – I'm just not completely sure why. I can probably clear it up in two questions though. Fancy seeing how the other half live?"

....

Within the hour, Watson found himself standing on the door step of Jimmy Jones' mansion. Expensive sports cars adorned the gated driveway and when Holmes pressed the ornate doorbell, it rang out to the tune of a popular chant from the terraces of Jones' premiership club. One of the household staff ushered them inside. The interior was as Watson had expected, ultra-modern and what could only be described as 'a bit naff'. In the sitting room, professional pictures were hanging on the walls of Jones and his now-wife, posing together seductively, her ample chest and his massive gold watch clearly on display.

The man himself finally entered the room, looking agitated and tired. He offered his guests a seat but Holmes declined.

"Do you suffer from psoriasis Mr Jones?" he asked, abrupt and to the point as usual.

"No, I don't. Glad though, it's well bad. You can get it, like, everywhere on your body. Why are you here? Have you found Kathy? Has she said something to you?"

"And toiletries Mr Jones, you have a sponsorship deal with a leading brand – is that right?"

"Yeah, and?"

"Do they supply you with all you need or do you ever use any other brand – fragrance, shaving products, skincare?"

"No, they send me loads of the damn stuff, more than I could ever use. Never use nothing else. Why? What's this all about? Have you found her?"

"Thank you Mr Jones. That's all I needed to know."

....

The following evening saw Hopkins back at Baker Street in response to a summons from Holmes. Watson was there too, responding to an insistence from Defonte that if Kathy wasn't found in the next 24 hours, the publisher he was negotiating with would terminate the contract. Watson's eagerness to save the day, and with it his own failing writing career, made him decide to visit Holmes and keep him on track. Holmes was clearly delighted to have an audience; Watson had noticed many times during their friendship that Holmes liked a touch of the dramatic, particularly when there was someone there to appreciate it. There was room in his usual cold and controlled nature for a liking of flattery and praise, particularly when he elicited it from the often sceptical official police.

"Well, I hope your summons means that you've finally got some news for me Mr Holmes. When I received your text, demanding I be here for 8pm, I'd just had to release Mrs Tandy. Couldn't hold her any longer - no evidence. But all my instincts are telling me that she's involved. We have a strong motive and a suspect..."

"But no actual evidence and no Miss Rice. As ever Hopkins, your brilliance astounds me."

The young officer looked dejected and sat back down heavily upon the worn old sofa.

"Alright Mr Holmes, you better give me your take on things. But I don't see how you can be any closer to knowing where Miss Rice is than I am."

"Really, we'll see about that then." Holmes looked at his watch and there was a buzz on the intercom. "Right on time," he smiled.

"Miss Rice?" Hopkins exclaimed, jumping up from his seat.

"No, your prime suspect," Holmes replied, pressing a button on the intercom and asking Mrs Tandy to come up and join them.

Once she was settled into the fraying old arm chair, Watson brought Mrs Tandy a cup of tea and placed it into her shaking hand. She looked tired and fraught, lack of sleep and deep pain clearly etched onto her face. Hopkins simply looked astounded and sat in respectful silence as Holmes gently questioned her.

"Please, tell us about the affair Mrs Tandy, I know this must be painful but as I explained in the email I sent to you, full disclosure could be your only option to clear your name - regardless of the implications for others. This is why I asked you to come here. This is a safe place where you can put forward your side – I have special allowances from the police and they indulge my liking for hearing the truth in the comfort of my own home rather than a police interview room. I offer you my protection if you can tell me everything that you know."

"It's not me I'm worried about, it's my children and what this scandal will do to them once it gets out. That's why I've stayed silent, and I suppose after all these years I still have some loyalty. But clearly from your email you already know the truth so there's no point in me hiding it from you. Please, tell me Mr Holmes, how did you know about the affair?"

"Initially because of the wedding flowers. I noticed what an unusual choice they were as soon as I saw them. I made some enquiries with the florist who told me that Rico Tandy had chosen and paid for them – a wedding gift. But why chose carnations and Forget-me-nots for a wedding? Flowers normally associated with funerals. To your husband, this wasn't a wedding - it was a funeral after the death of an affair. Tell me, how bad is your husband's psoriasis? I noticed a little of it on his wrists when he first came to see me, but suspect it is much worse."

Slightly bemused Mrs Tandy rubbed her hand over her brow. "Yeah, it's pretty bad – all up his arms and shoulders. Uses cream for it, doesn't make much difference though. How is this relevant?

"There was a large tube of cream in Jones's room at the hotel. I remembered noticing that your husband was a sufferer and I know that Jones isn't. There were clothes too; a pair of trousers 36 inch waist, Mr Jones can only be a 28 at most. Rico must be at least a 36. And the toiletries, clearly they didn't all belong to Jones. He has a sponsorship deal with a leading skincare brand and they supply him with all he needs, but in the bathroom I found products by another brand. I've made a little study of how to identify different men's fragrances – I've got quite a nose for it now. The brand of grooming products was the same as the brand of fragrance your husband was wearing the night I met him."

"Alright, I don't want to hear any more. I get the picture." Mrs Tandy interjected weakly. "Perhaps if I had been so observant I would have worked out my husband was sleeping with Jones ages ago. But I trusted Rico, we've been married for ten years, got three kids together. I helped him grow his business. I thought we were a team. But it was all just lies, a terrible, hurtful sham to hide the truth – a truth which is career suicide in the macho world of professional football. Rico is gay. My whole marriage has been a lie."

She paused to wipe away a tear from her cheek then continued, "He came back to our house on the morning of the wedding and broke down in front of me, confessed everything. He had arranged this stupid wedding and called time on the affair with Jones but they spent one last night together, the night before the ceremony. He was heartbroken it was over, had been drinking and came home to me – the one person he had always turned to when in trouble. Jones is gay too but covers it up by shagging a stream of models and porn stars. They are both pathetic and I told Rico that, I screamed at him to get out of our house, never see our children again. I told him I'd take everything, break him. He sped off in his Porsche and I just collapsed in tears. I raided his drinks cabinet and drank my way through half of it. I had met Jones loads of times, had him round for dinner, for parties, to stay over with us. I suddenly became furious with him too – how could he be so normal to my face and be screwing my husband behind my back?

I went to the wedding, ready to tell all but he stopped me in reception and begged me not to. The security removed me and I felt so humiliated. I sat in the car park and must have passed out, I don't remember anything else until waking up in my car and realising the wedding would be over by now. Then I remembered that I had Kathy Rice's phone number stored in my mobile. I started to call her repeatedly, left her a message saying her new husband was a cheat. She called me back and I blurted out everything – thought she had a right to know. She was furious, called me a liar but I knew she believed me. I hung up and went home. I did nothing to her and have no idea where the stupid cow is. The only thing I'm guilty of is drink-driving."

Hopkins insisted that he take Mrs Tandy to the station for further questioning but Holmes asked for a slight concession.

"Let her stay here with Watson and I promise that if I have not convinced you of her innocence within the next hour, I will accompany her to the station myself."

"Holmes, I really should be getting back, my wife..." Watson interjected.

"But this gives Mrs Tandy an even stronger motivation for revenge on Jones. Until we find Miss Rice, she remains a suspect and should be back in police custody. Remember the ripped wedding dress? Clearly there has been an angry physical altercation and right now I can think of no one with better motive. Alright, I'll give you an hour," agreed Hopkins, "but after this revelation I dread to think what else you have in store Mr Holmes."

....

The hotel manager was obliging as always and listened to Holmes' request. Upon seeing Hopkins' warrant card, he readily found the necessary room key and let them both up the grand staircase.

"I don't understand what we are doing here Holmes," asked Hopkins as they mounted the stairs. "Why are we at the hotel?"

"Because Watson made an excellent point last time we were here. He asked how one of the country's most recognisable women could leave without being seen – especially in that God-awful frock. It played on my mind so I came back this afternoon and checked the guest-list. Something jumped straight out at me and made everything clear."

They were standing outside room 34. The manager knocked on the door then swiped a card into the lock. Holmes opened the door and strode into the room. There, sitting on the bed watching television was a young woman.

"No one saw her leave simply because she didn't leave, did you Miss Rice?" asked Holmes, as the startled glamour model jumped up from the bed in surprise. Her best friend came out of the bathroom and gasped to find two strange men standing in her hotel room. "Who are you?" she asked. "Did he send you?"

"I am Sherlock Holmes and this is Detective Inspector Hopkins of Scotland Yard."

"The police?" said Kathy in surprise. "What's anything got to do with you lot?" she asked in a broad Essex accent.

"Are you even aware that you have been reported missing?"

"I'm not missing, what you on about? Is that what he thinks? My so-called husband? Yeah well, I am missing to him. So bloody missing he'll never see me again!"

"She's just lying low for a bit, staying in my room for a few days until Jimmy gets the message and leaves her alone."

"If I'm missing, then how come you've found me Mr whatever-your-name is?"

"It's part of my job – to find people who don't want to be found. When I saw on the guest list that your closest friend was still staying at the hotel two days after the wedding, even though all the other guests had checked out, I suspected that you were hiding out in her room. I knew you had to be here somewhere because no one saw you leave. I spent an industrious afternoon making enquiries amongst all the wedding guests and hotel staff, I thoroughly checked all security tapes of the exits, gardens and car park. No sign of you. The only remaining conclusion had to be that you hadn't left at all. Seeing that Miss Beaton was still staying here rounded off my theory rather nicely."

"But why was your wedding dress torn and floating in the Thames?" asked Hopkins, his brain frantically working to keep up – and trying to look anywhere other than Miss Rice's generously enhanced features.

"In the Thames?" Kathy exclaimed in surprise, turning to her friend. "I told you to get rid of it, not float it down the Thames where the whole of London could see it!"

"Sorry hun I wasn't thinking."

"I couldn't stand to look at it. I was so angry that I ripped it to pieces and asked Candice to get rid. Thought she's be a bit more cleverer than that though."

"Alright, whatever. It ain't my fault your husband's a bender, babes. Oh, I mean, you know, a gay person."

"Sod that political correctness nonsense, I've called him much worse. I ain't got no problem with gay blokes but not when they're shagging me as well! Does everyone know now? Have the press got hold of it? That's another reason why I'm hiding away – can't bare the shame of it. 'Kathy Rice marries gay footballer' – I can just see the headlines. I mean, I know this wedding was a publicity stunt – I never thought it was a great love affair but he said he really fancied me, we were having sex. How could he do that to me? How could he do that at all if he was gay?" Kathy started to cry, black mascara smudging from her false eyelashes.

"It's ok sweetie, everyone will think he's mad to choose that fat manager over you," cooed Candice trying to be helpful but actually making Kathy sob even louder.

Holmes was clearly uncomfortable with such displays of emotion and eager to leave now that he had revealed Miss Rice's whereabouts to Hopkins. He assured the girls that the press were still in the dark about the whole business and urged Miss Rice to come out of hiding and front it out.

"I've got lots of front Mr Holmes," she added cheekily, a little of her old sparkle starting to return.

....

"I knew the dress had been torn in anger by Miss Rice herself," said Holmes over the gentle sound of choral music rising from his sound-system back at 221b. Watson needed to get back to his wife but was desperate to know all the final details of the case. They were alone now – Hopkins had offered to take Mrs Tandy home and agreed that she was not to face any charge. Now that the case was concluded, Holmes was clearly bored of it already and starting to lose himself in the music enveloping the room. "Quite simply, if it had been ripped during a scuffle it would have blood on it,

DNA. You'd have to be pretty stupid if you were the attacker to just throw it into the river."

"But what about-"

"Not now Watson, it's late and all my energies have drained. You are welcome to stay but please do so in silence."

"Oh, right, I might as well go home to the wife then. She'll be asleep by now; she won't want to talk to me either. Shout at me possibly, but I'm getting rather used to that."

....

The next time Larry Defonte called Watson at work, it was an altogether better conversation. Watson's original publisher was interested in offering him another book deal. They were suddenly keen to see more of his adventures with the fascinating Mr Sherlock Holmes, as long as this included his write-up of Miss Rice and her wedding to premier bachelor Jimmy Jones. Defonte wanted to know if Watson would agree to reveal all about Holmes' involvement. As the story of Jones' sexuality was already out in the public domain after a press feeding frenzy, Watson didn't see what harm it could do. Rico and Jones had openly rekindled their relationship, though Jones had been stuck on the subs bench and eventually taken a contract with a football team in China.

Why shouldn't I take a slice of the pie?" thought Watson as Defonte waited on the end of the line for an answer. "I'll do it," he replied, and genuinely relished another opportunity to show the nation why there really was something very special about Sherlock Holmes. And if it made him some money and pleased his wife along the way, all the better. Besides, it was the perfect excuse to buy a new watch.

The Leaping Man

Everyone told him not to worry about it. He even told himself not to worry. But Gareth Lestrade couldn't throw the pictures away. He was looking at them again now, the newspaper spread out on the bed he shared with his gorgeous young girlfriend. Was it just the poor lighting that made him look so old, caught by the paparazzi leaving a club with her at 3am? Was it the unflattering angle or the fact that he'd been awake for almost 24 hours? No, he concluded, it was simply age that made him look so haggard and no excuse would convince him otherwise.

"I thought I told you to get rid of them?" Della remonstrated, walking out of the en-suite, her expensive pink underwear emphasising her perfect figure and tan. "Babe, you've just got to forget about it. I've had loads of bad pictures in the press over the years," she purred in her warm Northern accent. He hurriedly scooped up the paper from the bed and pulled his dressing gown tightly around his bare middle-aged body.

"You don't understand." He tossed the paper into the bin.

"Gareth, you're being ridiculous."

He stormed from the bedroom closing the door heavily behind him. She would never understand.

Doctor Watson knew all about arguing with a partner. So he listened to Della's story with interest and thought of the times he had considered running away. Not that his wife would even notice. Or care. She certainly wouldn't consult Sherlock Holmes for help as Della was doing now. She'd be more likely to pay someone to keep him away. And she thought Holmes was a moron who he should have grown out of by now.

"Please Mr Holmes, you helped before and I know you can help me again," Della pleaded, sitting neatly on the sofa at 221b. "No one is taking my concerns seriously. They all think he's run off somewhere because we've been arguing so much. But I know Gareth. He wouldn't do that to me and he certainly wouldn't abandon his job. He's still my security manager and he's so professional, whatever has happened between us as a couple would never affect that."

Sherlock Holmes looked bored. "You've contacted the police I presume?"

"Yes, but when they checked the records, his bank card has been used and his phone. They think the same as everyone else, he's just left me."

"Well then," replied Holmes matter-of-factly, "at least you know he's not dead."

"So where the hell is he and why won't he contact me?" replied Della angrily, getting up from the sofa, her large blue eyes filling with tears.

Holmes was distracted by something outside the window which had caught his eye.

"You are afraid of something. You have changed security as a result."

"How do you know?"

Holmes was looking down to the street below. "The protection officer you have with you today is twice the size of the man in this picture," he leafed through a massive pile of old newspapers scattered at his feet and pulled out the photos which had started all the arguments between Della and her much older boyfriend. "The protection officer with you and Lestrade in this picture is quite slight. He's also unarmed. The brute outside my front door is huge with a holster clearly showing through his jacket."

"Yeah, well, there have been a few incidents but it's a separate issue. All I care about is finding Gareth. It's been two weeks since he went out one morning and never came back. I know something's not right Mr Holmes. Stalkers and nutcases I can deal with, it's all part of being a celebrity, but not losing Gareth – the daft, stubborn old sod means everything to me. I'm not bothered about his age, or how he looks in a few dodgy photos. I just want him home."

"He left of his own free will, took credit cards, phone – which he has used since – and is an adult, free to come and go as he pleases. I don't know what you are expecting me to do. You just said it yourself, he's stubborn. If he's chosen to leave, I doubt there's anything anyone can do to bring him back until he's ready."

"So you think he's left me too, just like everyone else. Well, great. Thanks for nothing. Maybe everyone is right. Typical though - he was so insecure, going on about how I'd 'come to my senses' one day and leave him for someone my own age. And now it looks like he's gone and left me instead!"

Della started to cry. Watson tried to diffuse the situation by offering a cup of tea.

"Typical English thing to do," she replied. "Have a brew to make everything better. Except it don't work."

"I prefer cocaine, it works rather well," remarked Holmes.

After an awkward silence, Watson laughed nervously.

"He's joking, of course," he added - unconvincingly.

....

After signing off documentation for yet another 'crash-for-cash' person, Doctor Watson sat at his desk and worked his way through a large bar of chocolate. "I'm putting on weight," he thought. "Comfort eating," he added, scoffing down another square and opening the newspaper. He couldn't work out which bored him the most, his job or his life. Or was it just a midlife crisis? He had yet to hear back from his literary agent regarding a new book deal; in fact Defonte wasn't even returning his calls. This was not a good sign and the black clouds of doubt and depression had begun to circle again.

His introspection was rapidly interrupted when he saw Della's picture staring out from the pages. "Oh my God!" he exclaimed, grateful for an excuse to abandon his desk and rush out to hail a cab to Baker Street. He was past caring whether the lawyers he worked for in 'no-win-no-fee-hell' sacked him. He only took the job to keep his wife happy and even that hadn't worked.

Any hopes he had of surprising Holmes with this new information were shattered when Watson burst into the sitting room at 221b and found Della sitting opposite his friend in a very agitated state.

"Your timing is perfect Watson, I think Miss Breton is in need of a sedative,"

"You forget Holmes, I'm not a proper doctor anymore – no bag of potions. Just assist lawyers helping people to defraud their insurers. Calls for nothing accept a lack of morals I'm afraid. I read about what happened and came straight over."

He sat beside Della, feeling the old excitement flooding back and making him miss the days when assisting Holmes was his full-time occupation.

"It's the stalker Mr Holmes, after what happened last night I'm convinced he's a jealous nut-job and has done something to Gareth. After the way he attacked Diamond Dude, he clearly doesn't want any other man near me."

"Perhaps for the benefit of Watson, you could describe again what happened last night?" Holmes asked, his soothing voice calming the troubled pop-star. "The account in the paper was typically sensationalist."

"My new management company have arranged for me and the band to do a collaboration with US rapper Diamond Dude, or Colin Smith if you want his real name. I know, bit of a difference. It's a great opportunity; he's a really big star. He's flown over from LA with his entourage. Me and the girls have been asked to entertain him while he's here, get shots of us together in the papers. So we took him to this really exclusive, members-only club last night. He acts like a bit of a prat but he's alright really. We were getting on ok; I even managed to have a bit of a laugh despite everything. Then suddenly, this nut-job appears out of nowhere, grabs my drink and throws it to the floor. He drags The Dude away from me and starts hitting him. Colin's a big bloke but he still managed to tackle him to the ground. It was awful, people were screaming and the madman was in such a rage.

I thought he was going to attack me too. It's been coming for a while, he's been following me, even started raging at a guy the other week who rushed at me for an autograph."

"Can you describe the man?" Watson asked.

"Every time I see him he's wearing a hoodie and a scarf covering most of his face. He's clearly not right in the head though, his mannerisms are all weird. He sort of...jumps about. Like a frog. It's really freaky."

"Jumps?" asked Watson for clarification.

"Yeah, I know. Total head-case. The police are looking into it. I can't believe all this is happening; especially now I'm without a security manager. What if the jumping man is an obsessed fanatic who's purposely got Gareth out of the way?"

Holmes was out of his seat now and pacing the floor. He turned to Della.

"Go," he commanded abruptly, "there is nothing more you can tell me. I will send for you when I need you."

"But, what do you mean? Are you going to look for Gareth or not?"

"Not. Now, if you'll excuse me, I have an appointment for a beauty treatment."

Watson never ceased to be shocked by his friend's unusual manner and odd revelations. But this one was particulary surprising. Incredulous, Della angrily marched towards the door.

"Thanks for nothing. You know, I actually thought underneath that cold and frankly odd exterior, there was a pretty decent bloke. Clearly, I thought wrong." And with that parting comment, she swept from the room.

....

The following morning at work, Watson sat through the disciplinary hearing with gritted teeth. He wanted to tell the lawyers exactly what he thought of them and their boring job but just wanted it to be over quickly. So, he agreed with everything they said and apologised as convincingly as possible for disappearing from his office for half a day without permission. He also apologised for his general lateness, lack of commitment and for telling a claimant to 'sod off'. Fortunately his contrite manner worked well and the lawyers speedily agreed to give him one more chance, sending him home for the rest of the day to reflect on his behaviour. This meant he could rush straight to Baker Street, catch up on the investigation and still be home in time for dinner – if he was late for that again his wife would pull him into a disciplinary. And she was far scarier than the lawyers.

....

"You've been drinking", Holmes remarked as Watson entered the room.

"How can you possibly know that?"

"From the gum wrapper stuck to the bottom of your shoe."

"Ok," Watson smiled, settling into his usual chair, "explain?"

Holmes did enjoy showing off his unusual abilities and had a love of flattery which was at odds with his otherwise rather unemotional demeanour. He was just about to explain his reasoning when Watson made a surprising observation of his own.

"Your face looks different," he stated.

"Restylane, a dermal filler - I've had it injected into my forehead."

"Have you lost your mind?"

"No, just a few frown-lines. Now, we have a night's work ahead of us. Will you come?"

"One day, I'll come to visit you and we'll just have a normal conversation – talk about the weather maybe, things in the news, relationships. But clearly not today. Ok, let's descend further into the realms of the strange. Does the work have anything to do with Della and her jumping man?"

"If you wanted normal Watson, you'd have stayed at home with your wife."

"Well, I do have to get home for dinner. Then, I'm all yours."

"She'll know you've been drinking. Your breath still smells despite chewing the gum to disguise it."

....

Much later that evening, Watson returned to Baker Street, dressed smart-causal just as Holmes had instructed. He was surprised to find his friend wearing a very trendy shirt, skinny trousers and a hint of aftershave. All of which worked well with his newly smoothed forehead.

"Holmes, its fine if you are but, I have to ask, are you turning gay?"

"Happy gay or homosexual gay?"

"Fillers in your forehead type of gay."

"Come on, time to go clubbing."

"A gay club?"

"Oh Watson, sometimes you are slow to catch on old friend. You really have no idea about this investigation do you?"

"So, are we going to a nightclub to catch Della's jumping stalker or just because you want to show off your new face?"

"Well, I do look remarkably young but this evening is about business not pleasure."

....

Watson hadn't set foot in a nightclub for years. The first thing he noticed was how loud it was. The second, how much older he was than everyone else there. Holmes looked perfectly comfortable. He had the most remarkable ability to fit in anywhere – as long as he wanted to. He was adaptable, like a chameleon. A big advantage for all the times he needed to be seen but not seen.

A bouncer checked their names against a list then ushered them to the VIP area. Once inside, Watson marvelled at the beautiful people dancing and sipping expensive Champagne. He recognised a few from TV and felt suddenly rather star-struck – and very out-of-place. Then he saw Della sitting in a group towards the corner. He recognised two of the girls from her band and presumed that the massive bloke sitting next to her wearing a baseball cap was The Dude. He had an entourage of black-suited men and scantily clad women milling around him as he whispered something in Della's ear. She looked stunning in a short black dress, bare tanned legs and ridiculously high heels. Her cropped blonde hair sparkled in the flashing lights. Watson concluded that Lestrade was absolutely mad to leave her but understood completely why he felt he had to.

Holmes did not approach Della and her party, but steered Watson to a table far enough away that they wouldn't be noticed but could watch everything that was going on.

"Diamond Dude flies back to LA tomorrow. This is his last chance to make his move," Holmes shouted in Watson's ear.

"I thought we were here to catch Della's stalker?"

Holmes sat back in his seat, drink in hand and a look of intense concentration on his face. He didn't take his eyes off Della for the next two hours. Watson thought he was looking at her slender crossed legs but as time passed, he realised that his attention was actually focused on the low table she was sitting at and her drinks on top of it.

By midnight, Watson was pretty tired and knew his wife would be home from her sister's by now. He was going to be in so much trouble when he got back. Then, suddenly, Holmes grabbed his wrist.

"Now! Quickly!" he shouted, pulling Watson to his feet. "Take her glass and keep hold of it whatever happens," he commanded, signalling towards Della.

As they rushed up to her, Watson snatched the wine glass from her hand just as someone else was about to do the same. The man tussled with him until Holmes took a firm hold and started to drag him away – even though he was fidgeting and jumping around like a man possessed.

"The game is up, I know who you are," Holmes said to him. "Watson, give the glass to the inspector."

"Who? What's going on Holmes?" Watson asked, perplexed.

Della was on her feet now. Watson turned to see the familiar face of Detective Inspector Hopkins standing beside him. Confused, he did as Holmes had asked and passed him the glass. By now, The Dude was on his feet and trying to slip away. Hopkins instructed his sergeant to give chase and soon the big rapper was safely handcuffed, shouting obscenities.

Holmes had a tight grip of the jumping man – a curious sight in a hoodie with a scarf covering all but his eyes. Eyes that looked strangely familiar.

"Will you please explain to me what this is about?" Della asked Holmes.

Holmes hesitated long enough for her to snatch the scarf from the face of her stalker. She gasped in complete shock. "Gareth!" she cried, "Oh my God, what the bloody hell's going on?"

Holmes released his grip, causing Gareth to twitch and then jump involuntarily. The embarrassment on his face was pitiful. Startled and hurt, Della shied away from him. "Stay away from me, just stay away," she shouted as her stunned band-mates looked at their security manager with a mix of horror and bewilderment.

"We should go," Holmes urged, "our work here is done." He patted Watson on the shoulder. "Let's return to the quiet sanctity of Baker Street and I will explain everything. We should leave Lestrade to do his own explaining."

....

"It all started with this," Holmes began once they were back at 221b. He tossed the newspaper across to a rather tired

Watson – for whom the adrenaline of the previous hour had slipped away leaving only sleepiness and fear of his wife's rage in its place.

Watson looked at the pictures of Lestrade looking past his best.

"No, not the pictures," Holmes interrupted, "the advert at the bottom of the page."

Watson looked down and saw a small advert for a Harley Street clinic promising 'The latest innovation in anti-aging treatments'.

"I'm too tired to figure it out Holmes, and I'm sure the music has made me deaf in one ear. I really am getting too old for all this excitement. Can you speak up a bit?"

"When Della first told me Lestrade was missing and showed me that picture which had started all their arguments, my attention was drawn instantly to the advert. The fact that Lestrade was still using his bank cards and phone suggested strongly to me that he had simply gone off to have a procedure done and was lying low until the surgical wounds healed. He already had insecurities about his age and that photo pushed them to breaking point. I imagine he studied it many times and would surely have seen the advert below. The clinic's website is very impressive; enough to lure an insecure middle-aged man into parting with his cash. So, I booked myself in for a treatment to investigate further. Therapists can be so indiscrete, especially when it comes to celebrity gossip. It wasn't difficult for me to find out that pop-star Della Breton's boyfriend had tried one of their newest innovations – an injection of bull-frog serum, a powerful peptide with antioxidant properties.

When Della told me she had a stalker, I already suspected that her dedicated boyfriend-come-security-manager had not fully abandoned his duties. He wanted to keep an eye on her but didn't want to be seen – hence the hoodie and scarf. He had already intervened with an over-zealous autograph hunter, but what I didn't understand was why he had attacked a man she was collaborating with. Why do something which would be potentially harmful to her career? So, I did a little research into our friend The Dude and when Della told me about the stalker smashing her glass – all became very clear."

"Well, maybe to you Holmes. It's still muddy waters as far as I can see."

Watson's phone rang for the hundredth time since they had returned to Baker Street.

"Perhaps you should answer that?" Holmes asked, clearly irritated by the interruption.

"God no, it's the wife. Believe me, it's best if I don't."

Homes rolled his eyes impatiently then continued –

"Diamond Dude was arrested last year for allegedly spiking the drink of a female model, someone who had previously rebuffed his advances. He didn't do it himself of course; he got one of his entourage to slip Rohypnol into her Vodka. Despite their insistence that he was the real culprit, the young man was sent down in his place.

It is clear from interviews given since his arrival here that Colin Smith is interested in more than just Della's singing voice. But even he knew there was no chance of seducing her because of her devotion to her current partner. So, believing him to be out of the way, he felt safe to try the chemical method. But of course, Lestrade saw him and smashed the glass before Della could drink it. Pumped up on testosterone shots – another speciality of the clinic meant to rejuvenate vigour, Lestrade's anger spilled over into the physical altercation Della described.

As it was a private members' club, the stalker had to be a member to get access – this also confirmed my suspicions that the man was Lestrade. In his capacity as security manager he would obviously have membership to all the same clubs as Della and the band.

Knowing that tonight was The Dude's last night in London, I was reasonably sure he would try another attempt to secure Della's interest. I also knew that Lestrade would be there to stop him. Della confirmed that she would be seeing Colin Smith tonight, told me which club and arranged for us to have access to the VIP area. I asked for Hopkins and his team to be at the club and gave the signal as soon as I saw the drug go into the drink. I think that makes everything clear."

Watson's head was spinning with all this new information, not to mention the wine he'd been on all night and the ringing in his ears.

"But what about the jumping? It was ridiculous, like some sort of horrible nervous twitch."

"The bull-frog serum. A nasty side affect I'm afraid and the real reason why Lestrade couldn't come home. He couldn't possibly hide it from Della and was far too embarrassed to tell her the truth. It wasn't marks from surgery that kept him away - it was the frog-like behaviour and nasty temper brought on by the testosterone. It will all wear off in time of course, but until then I can't blame him for wanting to lie-low. Whether the damage to his relationship will wear off quite so quickly is another matter. If only he had gone for the Restylane like me. I couldn't be happier with the results. And I'm able to keep my feet firmly on the ground."

....

Watson called Defonte's number and left him yet another message. He sent him an email too. He wanted to be the type of person who was 'cool' about this sort of thing, didn't chase or pester but waited for people to come to them, the type of person who was confident in their own talents. People like Sherlock Holmes. But instead he was needy, a bit desperate and distinctly un-confident. Or cool. And he was facing a working lifetime stuck in 'no-win-no-fee-hell'. That call from his agent couldn't come soon enough.

A Question of Identity

"Do you see much of Lestrade?" asked Detective Chief Inspector Gregson while pouring himself more tea from the pot. "She threw him out you know, that pop star he was shacked up with. Don't know why, papers just said they had a bust-up over something and she sent him packing. Can't say I'm surprised, punching well above his weight there."

"Did you come here for something specific Gregson or just to indulge in a little idle gossip?" Holmes asked impatiently.

It was no secret that Lestrade and Gregson had been professional rivals at Scotland Yard and there was no love lost between the two men. Gregson had been promoted to DCI since Lestrade's departure and had come out of the 'Sherlock Holmes scandal' quite well. Lestrade had been made the scapegoat and though Gregson had used Holmes' services himself on various occasions, once the scandal broke he blamed it on Lestrade, saying that he had been pressured into using Holmes on his advice. He had felt quite smug about shafting his rival and scoring a promotion, but finding out that said rival had gone on to get a top job in security and move in with a 29 year old pop-star, rather took the edge off things. He was now clearly gloating over his ex-colleague's change of fortune.

"Well, obviously I'm not here in any sort of official capacity, I'm simply in the area and thought I'd catch up with an old acquaintance. It's been a long time Holmes."

Gregson settled back into the sofa nursing his mug of tea.

"Though," he added wistfully, "I am involved with a rather perplexing case at the moment, something right up your street. I'd be happy to have a casual, non-official chat with you about it, if you are interested. And then if you had any opinions on the matter perhaps you could share them – off record, as it were..."

Holmes didn't like indirectness. He was starting to find Gregson rather annoying and wished he hadn't offered him that cup of tea. Thank goodness Watson hadn't brought him a plate of biscuits too or they would never get rid of him, Holmes thought as Gregson eased even further into the cushions.

"Very well Gregson. Just get on with it and give me the details," said Holmes, not even trying to hide his irritation.

"Great, well, here are the facts of the case. A 14 year old girl has gone missing. Miss Priya Kumari, lives with her mother and step-father in Birmingham. Her father lives here in London – that's how we've got involved. He's a surgeon at The Royal London Hospital. They divorced three years ago – he's a practicing Muslim, very traditional. The mother, well, she's more westernised, new husband is white-British. Things are pretty amicable between both parties for the sake of the daughter. She's a good girl, never been in trouble. Very academic; wants to be a doctor like her father. Set off supposedly for school three days ago. No one's seen her since. Tried all the usuals; friends, other family members, etcetera, but drawn a blank. Her mum found this note left on her pillow," he handed Holmes a neatly handwritten letter on a folded sheet of note paper. It read simply – 'Dear Mum, don't worry about me. It's just something I've got to sort out. Will be back very soon. Love you, Priya.'

Holmes held the paper up to the light and examined it carefully with his magnifying glass. "Ripped out from a spiral-bound jotter pad, one that's well used judging by the condition of the paper. There is indentation from words written on other pages. Have forensics looked at this?"

"Yes. Only prints on there belonged to Priya and her mother. There was perfume too and a smudge of make-up. They didn't pick up on the other writing though," he added, with some embarrassment.

Holmes rolled his eyes but didn't look exactly surprised.

"I have become rather an expert on identifying different brands of perfume. This one is expensive, not something you buy with pocket money. Internet – has anyone checked her computer, Facebook account etc?"

"No," Gregson added. "Mother insists she's not on social media. They only have one laptop in the house which they all share. We've checked it and there's nothing on there of interest."

"What about her phone? She had internet access through that perhaps?"

"She took it with her. Clothes are missing from her wardrobe, make-up, hair straighteners, toiletries and money from her savings tin."

"Very well Gregson," said Holmes in a rather self important manner, "I will help you – discreetly. I will start by talking to her mother, if you can arrange a meeting."

"Great! Thank you. So, what do they say? The words from other pages? Do they give us a clue?"

"All in good time. My help, my rules."

....

Priya's mother was visibly shaken by the disappearance of her only child. Watson's wife was also very shaken by the news that her husband would be bunking off work to spend the day in Birmingham – just when she hoped he was starting to settle down. In reality, he was checking his phone every five minutes waiting for a call from Defonte, waiting for that life-changing phone call all would-be writers dream of. He was waiting to hear whether a major book deal was in the offing, one that would enable him to give up the day-job and begin his life as a professional, full-time writer. He could see it all now – the book signing tours, the posters in bookshop windows, the interviews in the press, maybe even the opportunity to travel. Though the first book hadn't exactly reached these heights, surely being a twice published author would be a game-changer? Settling down was the last thing on his ambitious mind.

As a medical man, Watson couldn't help but be concerned by how frail Priya's mother looked. Her husband, on the other hand, was quite robust. He sat with a possessive arm around his wife and insisted on jumping in and answering Holmes' questions himself.

"I'm sorry, but who did you say you was again? That copper said you might be able to help find her but you ain't the police are you?" he asked in a Birmingham accent. "So what's it got to do with you? Why should we tell you anything? I've only let you in 'cus the missus insisted."

Holmes ignored him and picked up a school photo in a frame.

"When was this taken?" he asked.

"About six months ago," the mother replied quietly. "It's not a very good school. Priya is so bright. That's why I agreed to her moving in with her dad. Just for term-time, so that she could go to a top school in London. He was happy to pay and she passed all the entry exams."

"When is she due to leave? Its October now, shouldn't she have started in September?"

"She changed her mind – was all for it to begin with, really excited about going to a good school to improve her chances of studying medicine at university. It was heartbreaking for me but I just wanted what was best for her."

"Well," interjected the step-father angrily, "how you could think it was best for her to live with that strict, old fashioned man you once had the misfortune to marry, I'll never know. She was fine here with us. Why did he have to start meddling? Fillin' her head with all these silly ideas about posh schools. Ain't nothing wrong with the schools around here. Didn't do me no harm."

"Mark didn't think she should go. Her father, my ex husband, is very strict you see. Very traditional. Mark thinks he would have pushed her too hard with homework, exam results. I suppose he would have, but Priya and her father have always been so close. She didn't mind all that, she loves her studies anyway. Or, she always did. They are both very academic."

"So, why did she change her mind?" Watson asked, slowly piecing together the details in his mind, knowing that Holmes was probably several paces ahead by now.

"She saw sense," grumbled Mark.

"Mark please, you're not helping," the mother urged, turning to Holmes with her tired eyes. "She began to have arguments with her father. She's growing up and he finds it difficult to accept."

"I don't blame the kid. He's too strict, always going on at her. Perhaps you should be questioning him instead. Or perhaps you should be out there looking for her not wasting time with stupid questions."

With that final comment, Mark snatched the photo from Holmes' hand and signalled for them to leave. Watson was more than happy to get out of there. There was something odd about the step-father's manner, he seemed to be just as controlling as the ex husband he clearly despised.

．．．．．．

"Notice anything strange about the photo?" Holmes asked, as they sat on the train heading back to the capital.

"Holmes, why do you ask me these things when you know the answer will probably be a no?"

"I thought you might surprise me. Sometimes you do. Most of the time you don't."

"Thanks for that, full of praise as usual," Watson added sarcastically. "If I wanted criticism, I'd spend the day with my wife."

"Don't be offended. It's one of the things I admire about you Watson. Your predictability. I have enough surprises in my work, you give me something dependable. Something I can rely on. I give you an escape from the boredom of your work and by the sound's of it, your marriage. You need surprises, I need a touch of normality. This thing, this friendship thing we have - it's mutually beneficial."

"That might actually be the nicest thing you've ever said to me. The only nice thing in fact. But you are wrong, my marriage isn't boring. It's fine. Just having a rough patch at the moment."

"And you Watson, are a terrible liar."

．．．．．．．

Priya's father's house was very different to the home she shared with her mother and step-father. It was in a very desirable part of London, beautifully furnished. He was clearly a wealthy man. He quietly and politely answered all of Holmes' questions, offered tea and some expensive biscuits which Watson found particularly pleasant. He admitted that he was strict in some of his ways but that he loved his daughter terribly. He broke down in tears as he described her to Holmes, a situation Holmes found very unsettling. He was never comfortable with displays of emotion but his soothing voice put Mr Kumari at his ease once more.

"All I want is for her to be found safe and well. If she wants to live with her mother then that is fine. If she wants to come here that is fine also, though it is now too late for her to start school and because next year would be her final GCSE year, the school will not take new pupils at such a late stage. Sadly she has missed her chance but all I want is for her to be ok. I do push her with her studies but only because I know she is capable and could have such a bright future. I don't want her to be like that awful man my wife has married. He doesn't even work. Priya's mother works very hard in her job as a school secretary but earns little. He is always in and out of jobs. What example does that give Priya? I want her to get the best education, make something of her life. It is only because I love her so much."

....

Watson returned to work that afternoon and sat at his desk staring at his mobile phone, willing it to ring. He needed good news more than ever. Since returning from Birmingham he had thought often about the conversation with Holmes on the train. *Is my marriage boring? And if it is, what on earth do I do about it?*

....

Priya's school was a typical inner-city comprehensive - overcrowded and a bit run-down. Loud and rather intimidating children jostled along the packed corridor like a swarm of ants, big bags over their shoulders smacking into one another and causing regular foul-mouthed outbursts. Watson was very relieved that he hadn't taken his wife's advice and gone into teaching. She thought the profession had better prospects than his current job but looking at the mob in front of him, Watson thought that he would rather take his chances with the lawyers down in the fiery depths of 'no-win-no-fee-hell' than try to control this lot. He'd been bullied at school and had never forgotten how cruel children could be. Now he was just bullied at home.

"Why are we here?" he asked Holmes, "I thought Gregson and co had already spoken to Priya's teachers?"

"They did. Come on, we're not here to see the teachers. It's time to engage with the mob."

"Oh God, don't tell me we need to talk to this lot. They'll think we're ancient and uncool. They won't want to talk to us. And we might get stabbed."

"Nothing like a bit of stereotyping. And speak for yourself; I still look quite youthful thanks to my fillers. Don't worry, they'll want to talk to us..." he reached into a hold-all and pulled out a video camera, microphone and various other bits of equipment. "Nothing like the lure of fame and celebrity to get a bunch of teenagers to cooperate."

A smartly dressed woman had been fighting her way along the corridor towards them. Now she stood before them and warmly extended her hand.

"Mr Honeywell I presume?" she asked Holmes, "welcome to our school. I must say we are very excited about this. I'm Melanie Sampson, the headmistress. Hard to believe I know, but in my youth I fancied a pop career myself – was even in a band with a few friends." She giggled flirtatiously as Holmes turned on his most charming smile, while still holding on to her hand.

"Not hard to believe at all, in fact, you have a face the camera would love. If you have the voice to match then, well, all I can say is that the pop world's loss is clearly education's gain," Holmes cooed in a voice as sickly sweet as syrup. Watson cringed and wondered what on earth he had got involved in this time, and why Holmes didn't warn him about these things beforehand. *'Come to the school with me and take notes while I ask questions'* Holmes had said, and it sounded simple enough at the time, but Watson should have known that things were never that simple with Holmes. And if they were, he wouldn't enjoy them half as much.

Melanie led them to a classroom at the end of the corridor. Inside, a group of eager teenagers jumped to their feet as they entered – a look of wonderment on their faces.

"Right everyone, this is Mr Honeywell and..." she paused to look at Watson, "sorry, I didn't catch your name?"

"Erm..." Watson hesitated, not sure what to say as he hadn't been adequately prepped for whatever role it was he was expected to play.

"My videographer, Mr Watson," Holmes quickly added.

"Mr Honeywell and Mr Watson are from CEX Records. As I explained to you in class, CEX saw a video of your dance group on Facebook and have come to talk to you about featuring in the next Angel's music video. This is a very exciting opportunity, don't forget that you are representing this school as well as yourselves, so please make our guests feel welcome."

Five minutes later, they were alone with the star-struck youngsters. Holmes explained to them that he wanted to get a sense of their personalities and their lives; this would all be used to help shape the roles they would play in the pop video. He told them that he understood this was a difficult time for the group as one of their members, Priya Kumari, was currently missing. If they were to give him as much detail as they could about Priya too, he would ensure that she wasn't left out of the opportunity once she returned.

You clever sod, Watson thought as he listened to his friend effortlessly lying in order to get information. He busied himself with setting up the camera on a tripod and distancing himself from proceedings.

Once the camera was set up and Watson figured out how it worked, he filmed the group as Holmes encouraged them to start talking about themselves, their friendship with each other and their lives. The group of six friends had come together over their love of dance. Inspired by acts on TV talent shows, they'd formed the dance troop in the hope of auditioning for the biggest TV talent show of them all - UK's Got the Fame Factor. They explained how hard they practised and that the auditions were only a month away. Everyone was worried about Priya and whether she would make it back in time, but they were used to rehearsing without her because she often pulled out of rehearsals because she was studying. She was an 'amazing' dancer they all agreed, but was the shyest of the group and was happiest when they were just 'mucking about' together and not in front of an audience. Her dad was 'well strict in-it' and didn't know she'd joined the group.

Holmes asked about their boyfriends, did they mind that the girls might become famous and go off to see the world? They all chatted away about boys who liked them, boys they were dating, boys they'd 'shagged' and boys they wanted to 'shag'. "Did Priya have a boyfriend?" Holmes asked.

"There was this boy and he was like, oh my God Priya's awesome but she was like, no way," one of the young girls piped up. "He was hittin' on her loads but she wouldn't go out wiv' him. He was gutted. She used to be all prim an' that, but now she likes make-up an' stuff but she ain't had loads of boyfriends. So we was all dead shocked when this lad said she'd knocked him back cus she was seeing this other kid. We were like, no way, she's never said nothing to us and it can't be no one from this school cus we'd know about it. So then we started asking her and we thought maybe she's made him up just to get rid of that lad but no, she confessed everything. Said she had a boyfriend but her dad would kill her and she didn't want to say no more about it. Not from round here. Claims she met him on Facebook. Then we thought, oh my God, maybe it's an arranged marriage. That dad of hers is makin' her marry her cousin or something. In Pakistan or whatever. That's why she can't say nothing. We was thinking we should tell the police but didn't want to get her into trouble if we was wrong – you get me?"

Holmes asked if she knew the boy's name. "Nah," the girl added, "not his full name. She just called him Tommy."

....

"How did we get away with that?" asked Watson, packing away the camera after Holmes ended the fake casting session and the teenagers noisily left the room. "Surely you can't just turn up at a school pretending to be a record executive and they just fling open the doors unquestioningly?"

"Well, it didn't happen quite like that. I pulled in a few favours from our favourite pop-star, Della Breton. She asked her record company to vouch for us and send through all the necessary paperwork a day in advance. They were happy to help when I explained that the safety of a vulnerable young girl was possibly at stake."

"But what about that bunch of wannabes? They think you are going to turn them into stars. You've tricked them Holmes, and they are going to be really disappointed when they find out."

"Oh Watson, you and your morals. Don't fret about it. All the free backstage passes and VIP tickets Della's going to send them will soften the blow."

....

"I didn't know you were on Facebook?" Watson asked upon walking into the living room at 221b that evening and seeing his friend on the familiar social networking site.

"I'm not," Holmes replied without looking up. "But my alter-ego Millie Smith is. She's fourteen, likes boys, perfume, dance and goes to the same school as Priya Kumari."

"You're on facebook pretending to be a fourteen year old girl? Isn't that a bit creepy?"

"Not if it helps me find Priya. Ah! Now then, we have progress." He turned to Watson flashing a victorious smile. "She's just accepted my friend request."

....

"Just thought you'd like to know," said Gregson rather smugly. "We've taken the father in for questioning after a tip-off from the school. Some of Priya's friends reported to their teacher that he might have been arranging a marriage for her abroad. A forced marriage. It would make sense I suppose, him being so religious. We checked his phone records; he's been making lots of calls to Pakistan where his family are from. And then there's her passport. We asked her mother if it was still at her home but she said the father had asked for it during the summer. Turns out he'd taken Priya over to the homeland during the summer holidays and had never returned the passport. Chances are he took her over there to meet a prospective match. That's probably why she decided against moving in with him and why things had become so difficult between them." He puffed out his chest in a self satisfied manner, waiting for praise from the one man least likely to ever give it.

"Brilliant Gregson," said Holmes, "as usual your level of competence has revealed itself."

"Well, yes, I am rather pleased with how things are progressing," Gregson replied in a self-congratulatory tone. Watson simply sat back and waited for the cutting remarks which he could sense bubbling away beneath Holmes' warm and sickly smile.

"No real evidence, just a bit of hearsay and a healthy dollop of racial stereotyping thrown in for good measure. Yes, well done Gregson – brilliant. Level of competence stuck around where it usually is - pretty low. Now, if you'll excuse me I have some real investigating to be getting on with. I presume you have checked Priya's Facebook account?"

Visibly stung by the comments but determined not to show it, Gregson inhaled deeply and stood to leave. "The mother said she wasn't on social networking sites."

"And a fourteen year old girl tells her mother everything? I used to have my frustrations with Lestrade but right now, I'm really starting to miss him. Goodnight Gregson, I will have information for you tomorrow but until then, do yourself a favour and let Mr Kumari go. You won't find answers from him and you won't be any closer to finding Priya."

....

"Just answer me one question," asked Holmes, back in Birmingham at Priya's home after explaining to her mother that Priya was using her Facebook account via her mobile phone, news which she found both reassuring and surprising in equal measure. "Did you buy her the phone?"

"Yes. Well, it was Mark really. She broke her old one and I said she would have to wait until Christmas but he said I was being too harsh. I'm not very up on technology so he chose it for her. One of those smart phones. I never even thought about whether she would have internet access. Oh I've been so stupid. To think my little girl had this whole other life on the internet and I had no idea. Do you think she met someone on there Mr Holmes? A boy? Is that where she is now?"

....

The phone call came at the worst possible time. Watson was sitting at his desk after a dreary meeting with the dreadful lawyers. He was having one of those 'where did it all go wrong' moments and eating a massive chocolate muffin – which just made him feel even worse. When he saw Defonte's name come up on his mobile, his heart started to race. *Could this be it, the moment when everything changes and my life really starts?*

"John-boy!" Defonte's voice boomed, "how are you? Hope all is well in the land of legal aid? Anyway, look old boy, I need to come straight to the point. Just heard back from the publisher about your book deal – the one in which you talk about the whole 'Kathy Rice marries gay footballer' thing."

Watson felt his stomach tighten into a knot. He felt suddenly rather sick and regretted the muffin more than ever. His hand start to shake and every fibre of his body tingled with anticipation, willing the next words to be what he'd waited so long to hear.

"So anyway, they've called up and its bad news old chum I'm afraid. It's a no-goer. They don't want to publish another book from you. Trouble is, Kathy Rice has been on every talk-show possible and already given all the details of what happened. And then there's Rico Tandy's wife, she's been doing the rounds of the press and chat-shows as well – pouring her heart out about her cheating husband and how he'd been secretly batting for the other team, so to speak. Anyway, they've decided to offer her a book deal instead – pretty impressive sum in the offing as well. Thank God she chose me to represent her, wouldn't have liked to have missed out on that. It's like I said to you before, celebrity sells. Ordinary middle-aged doctors don't I'm afraid. Sorry to be so blunt John old thing, but I can't go on representing you. You've had your five minutes of fame with your first book and you should be happy with that, it's more than most people get. All these people say 'oh yes, I've got a book or two in me' but they never do anything about it. You did, you got published and for a moment there it looked like you were going places. Give yourself a big old pat on the back for that. But I think it's time to stop now John. Dreams are great things but we all have to wake up sometime. Take this as your wake-up call matey."

Watson ended the call and sat in silence, a pile of claim forms in front of him, half a chocolate muffin and a note from one of the lawyers asking him if he could recommend something for his daughter's warts. For the first time in his adult life, John Watson actually cried – which just made him feel like even more of a failure than he already did.

Just before Holmes left Priya's house in Birmingham, he asked politely where he might find the bathroom. Priya's mother directed him up the stairs and he made his way along the landing. As he passed the master bedroom, he noticed a packed holdall on the bed. He sneaked quietly into the room not realising that Mark was behind the door pulling clothes out of his wardrobe.

"What the hell?" he asked angrily as Holmes startled him.

"Going somewhere?"

"What business is it of yours?"

"None, unless you have something to hide?"

"I've got a few days work up north."

"Manchester?"

"How do you know that?"

"The Manchester A to Z sticking out of your bag was a bit of a giveaway."

Holmes sat on the edge of the bed and looked at Mark with a thoughtful expression.

"It's convenient isn't it, Priya having an internet boyfriend who isn't local? She's never even met him has she? An innocent, gullible young girl who thinks that just because someone writes all this stuff on Facebook about how much he loves her, understands her etcetera, it's a genuine relationship. And because he's not local, she can't just turn up at his house or meet his friends to check."

"I don't know anything about that sort of stuff. I didn't know about a boyfriend. She talks to her mom about things like that not me."

"Except, it's not genuine is it? And now that Priya's false boyfriend has ended their false relationship, she's gone off to try and find him, make him change his mind. A vulnerable young girl alone somewhere is trying to find a person who doesn't even exist. And even a cruel manipulator like you feels a bit concerned for her. Not enough to tell the truth, but enough to go and look for her himself."

Mark swiftly shut the bedroom door and wrung his hands in agitation.

"Alright, alright, keep your voice down," he whispered. "I'll tell you everything but please don't tell the misses. You're right, I'm going to look for her. She'll be in Manchester somewhere. Oh God, what a mare. I didn't know she'd decide to run away, this wasn't meant to happen. Just thought she'd get over it. How can you be that broken hearted over someone you've never even met?"

....

Holmes got the call at midnight to confirm that, after following his instructions, Gregson and his team had found Priya staying in a hotel in Manchester. She had paid in cash and used her Facebook boyfriend's surname to check in - just as Holmes had suspected she would. With her make-up, perfect hair, expensive perfume and height, she had easily passed for someone eighteen.

She was taken to Scotland Yard for questioning and Gregson very reluctantly allowed Holmes to be present. Mainly because he didn't have a clue how Holmes had figured out where she was. Let alone why.

Priya confirmed that she had gone to Manchester to find a boy she had met on Facebook who claimed to live there – Tommy Styles. She had been having a 'relationship' with Tommy for the past three months even though they had never met face-to-face. As far as she was concerned, they were boyfriend and girlfriend and it was love. When he told her it was over and ended all contact, she was determined to find him and make him change his mind. Knowing that her mother would disapprove and in fear of her father finding out, she had kept the relationship secret and knew they wouldn't let her go to Manchester to find him. That's why she had run away without telling anyone where she was going or why. She didn't have an address for Tommy but she hoped that by hanging around the Trafford centre and other places he had mentioned, she might be able to track him down.

Holmes gently explained to the poor girl the cruel truth, a truth which he had suspected from when he first heard that she had met a boy on Facebook. He revealed the real identity of her internet love leaving her heartbroken and shocked. She asked to see her father and fortunately Gregson had followed Holmes' advice and let him go the day before. He came to collect her and was overcome with relief at seeing his daughter safe and well. But, he could not forgive the police for the terrible accusations they had made against him. Little did he know that his daughter's safe return was down to the work of an extraordinary amateur.

....

"But I don't understand," said Watson the next morning after dashing round to 221b before work in response to a text from Holmes telling him Priya had been found. His head was pounding from the terrible hangover brought on by an excessive bout of drinking the night before, and from his wife screaming at him when he crawled in at 3am to 'sort his life out'. "You need to start right at the beginning. Last time I spoke to you she was still missing. How did you know where to find her? Did you find out who Tommy was?"

"Consigned to the sofa last night?"

"How do you know that?"

"Creases made by the hard cushions on your face, the fact that you keep rubbing your old service injury which always plays up when your wife makes you sleep on the sofa and that fact that your breath stinks of alcohol – no one would want to share a bed with you smelling like that."

"He dropped me, Defonte. There's not going to be another book Holmes. So those fascinating abilities of yours won't be shared with the world after all. And I won't be a successful writer. Just a nobody. I knew my wife wouldn't understand so I went out, got pissed and just sort of drifted home at stupid-o'clock. So yeah, you're right. I slept on the couch. And I stink. Thanks for pointing it out. Any chance we can just talk about the case? I really don't want to think about my crappy life for a moment longer."

Holmes attempted to make a sympathetic face but it just didn't come out right. He didn't really know how to deal with this sort of thing. But he wasn't cold to his friend's suffering and managed a rather awkward squeeze of his shoulder, then offered him a cup of tea. Watson decided that he really must look in a dire state as it was the first time in all their years of friendship that Holmes had EVER offered to make him a cup of tea.

"It's ok Holmes, really. Just tell me about Priya, I know you're dying to. Start at the beginning though, because I can't make head nor tail of the whole thing."

Relieved at avoiding the tedious business of tea-making, Holmes sat in the tatty armchair which had come with the flat and looked as old as time itself, and began to explain everything.

"It was the photograph that gave me the first clue. Do you remember? The one at her mother's house – a school photo. It was only six months old and yet she looked very young, fresh-faced. No makeup on, hair not straightened. All very natural. A mere six months later, she's run away from home and left a note with make-up smudges on, perfume traces.

And she's taken hair straighteners with her. I looked at other pictures around the room, more recent ones. She's wearing fashionable clothes, quite grown-up ones. So, why does a fourteen year old girl suddenly become image conscious? It had to be a boyfriend."

"Is that why she was arguing with her father so much? I'm guessing he didn't approve of her wearing make-up. Or boyfriends"

"Exactly. And that was the point of the whole sorry business."

"I don't follow..."

"That house they lived in, it was expensive for a family with just one income. It might not have been exactly tasteful inside but it was pretty well kitted out – big flat screen TV, range cooker, expensive music system. They were living quite well on just a school secretary's wages. I got the father to give me details of how much maintenance money he pays each month for Priya, it's a tidy sum. No wonder her step-father didn't want Priya to move in with him. He would have stopped the payments if she was living under his roof. That was a lot of household income for the step-father to lose – he might even have to go and find a job of his own. He needed to find a way of stopping Priya from leaving home, of turning her against her father."

"Oh my God, are you saying..."

"On the note she left, I noticed words which had come through from other pages in the notepad. I could make out the letters TS with a heart shape drawn around them. I also saw the letters FB and suspected this might be Facebook. Her friends helpfully confirmed that she had a boyfriend who she had met on the social network site – someone who rather conveniently didn't live in the area. All this started to fit neatly into a theory that Mark had created a fake profile pretending to be a young boy and luring Priya into a relationship – one that would somehow prevent her from leaving home. I suspected she was using Facebook on her phone and set up a fake identity myself to try and get access to her wall. I knew I could only do this if we became Facebook friends. I messaged her saying I was a girl at her school who knew TS and had information for her. She accepted the request straight away and replied asking if I knew why he had broken up with her.

By flicking through the posts on her wall I could work out that she had been having an online relationship and his name was Tommy Styles.

Her mother confirmed that it was Mark who bought her the phone and Priya explained to the police that her step-father had introduced her to Facebook and helped her set up her own profile. He also bought her the expensive perfume, knowing her father would disapprove. 'Tommy' was fond of telling her how great she looked with make up on and encouraging her to disobey his strict rules. 'Tommy' also didn't want her to move to London because he was eighteen and had won a place at Birmingham University to study medicine. He told her to stay in Birmingham because they could soon be together. Once she told her father she wouldn't be moving in and lost her chance of ever studying for her GCSE's at the London school, it was time for Mark to end the 'relationship'. He broke off all contact and Tommy Styles disappeared forever, he had already served his purpose of keeping large monthly payments coming in to the household. That's when Priya decided to take off to Manchester, the place he alleged to be from, and find him."

Watson was shocked and lost for words, shocked by both Holmes' skill in solving the case and the cruelty of the step father towards an impressionable young girl. His military service had taught him plenty about the dark side of human nature and his experiences with Holmes had furthered that lesson.

"How did you know she was in Manchester?"

"Figured it out thanks to a well placed A to Z and a confession from Mark."

"But how did the police know where she was staying?"

"I knew she had taken money and her parents confirmed that she didn't have any friends or relatives in the city, so she must be in a hotel. From her glamorous profile picture, I could tell she would pass for a young adult. I suggested to

Gregson that he got his team to call all city centre hotels and find out if a Priya Styles was staying there. That's how they found her."

"Where is she now?"

"With her father. He telephoned me to thank me for my services. He was furious with the police for suspecting him of wrong-doing and is now livid that they didn't even solve the case. I wouldn't want to be in Gregson's shoes right now. There's an almighty official complaint heading his way. I don't think he'll be able to wriggle out of this one as easily as he did the last debacle. Priya's father called the London school first thing this morning and explained the situation to them. They have decided to make an exception and allow Priya to start the term after all. Her dreams of studying medicine are back on track and her father accepts that he will have to loosen the reigns a little now that she is growing up. She'll be fine. And if her mother has any sense she'll leave that good-for-nothing she married. He has broken no laws so the police can't do anything. She is the only one who can dish out any sort of punishment for his selfish actions."

"Interestingly, that might not necessarily be true," added Watson with a knowing smile. "I've been doing a little research myself. His surname is quite unusual – Birdwhistle. I knew I'd come across it somewhere before... Mark Birdwhistle. As you know, I work for a leading firm in the compensation business. We get claimants from all over the country choosing the firm because of all the TV advertising, posters etc. I checked the records and sure enough, a Mark Birdwhistle has got a claim going through at the moment. One of the other doctors had mentioned it because it was so obviously a scam but he was too afraid of his job to not sign off the forms."

Holmes leaned forward in his chair, suddenly full of interest.

"So, I decided it was time to do the right thing for once – to hell with the bloody lawyers. I got into the records department, found the papers and destroyed the forms the doctor had signed after his assessment of Mark's alleged injuries. I then filled out a new form giving him a clean bill of health. The case is being heard in the small claims court tomorrow. So long as no one notices until then, the court will see it and throw out his claim. He'll lose about £20,000. And I'll probably lose my job."

"Oh Watson, sometimes choices just have to be made and consequences lived with. You and your morals…"

"Yeah I know. I think the consequences for this could go beyond the professional though. That marital 'rough patch' I mentioned is about to get a whole lot rougher…"

Abbey Strange

"Look honey, it isn't really any of my business but I'm about to lose a bloody good security manager. I understand that it must be difficult working with your ex, but do I really have to accept his resignation or is there any way the two of you can sort things out? Della sweetheart, I know he hurt you and behaved like an idiot, but if I had a pound for every time my husband hurt me and behaved like an idiot, I'd be a billionaire instead of a plain old millionaire."

"Gareth's resigned?"

"Yes hun. Didn't he tell you?"

"No, we're not really speaking."

"If you genuinely want shot of him then fine, I'll have to let him go. But if you still love him, then perhaps you've punished him for long enough and it's time to give him another chance. Decide Della, because if not he'll be gone by the end of the month – been offered work in the States minding a Hollywood star. Gareth's one of the good ones Del - men like that don't come along often. The great thing about having a wise old crone like me for a manager is that you can learn from my mistakes. Sweetie, I know what it's like to be left crying over 'the one that got away'. Between you and me, I know more than ever right now."

Watson sat at his desk flicking through the newspaper. A cold draft blew in through the old windows and he sipped his steaming mug of coffee to take away the chill. The lawyers had plush offices on the upper floors with air con, posh carpets, smart furniture and panoramic city views. He was in the basement of the building, his view out of the window was a brick wall and his carpet was stained and threadbare. A morning glance through the papers brought a brief escape from his general misery, a chance to see other people's lives and how they were often much worse than his own. Like Tyler Welbourne for example, who now had no life at all.

The wrinkly rock-star had been murdered at his country mansion the previous night. It was front page news, the Welbournes were a high profile couple and the paper devoted pages to the incident. He was a drug-addled old rocker whose band, The Dreadful Death, had enjoyed big success during the 80s and 90s. His wife Karen had been their manager and stood by him despite the affairs, drugs and call-girls. She was now a powerful force in the music industry herself, a shrewd business woman who owed CEX Records and had taken over the management of girl-group The Angels, after the demise of the infamous Todd Carter. This made her Della Breton's manager and Lestrade's boss, something which made Watson particularly interested in the case. He was just about to call Holmes and ask if he had seen the news, when Julian Sinclair –Booth, partner in the law firm, walked into his office with a look of intense displeasure flickering across his aristocratic features. Watson closed the paper and braced himself – this wasn't going to be pleasant.

....

"Gareth, wait," Della called out, watching the back of her security manager disappear into the conference room. She rushed to catch up and walked in just as he was about to close the door.

"I'm doing a briefing in ten minutes," he said rather gruffly, taking folders from under his arm and spreading various documents out on the table. He didn't make eye-contact with her.

"I just wondered if you had heard from Karen. I've tried calling but she's not answering her phone. I just want to know if she's ok, if I can do anything to help. She's been so good to me and the girls. The papers say she was hurt too; the robbers tied her to a chair. She saw them kill her husband – God it's so awful, I can't imagine how she must be feeling. I know she can be a feisty cow but most of that is just an act."

Gareth looked up at his ex girlfriend and felt that terrible aching in his heart again which he couldn't get rid of. He was hoping the vast expanse of the Atlantic Ocean might help but seeing her standing there in the sweater he bought for her on a romantic break in Milan, running her fingers through her hair in the way she always did when anxious about something, he very much doubted it.

"I haven't heard from her. I'm going to head out there after this briefing, offer to help liaise with the police. Though I've heard she doesn't want to see anyone – which is understandable I suppose."

After some uncomfortably intense eye contact, Gareth swiftly returned to laying out his papers.

"We were talking yesterday; she said some odd stuff about crying over 'the one that got away' and how she knew how that felt more than ever."

"Why on earth did that come up in conversation?"

Della turned to look out across the city through the giant windows lining the walls. They were on the top floor of the record company headquarters, in a conference room designed to seriously impress. It was early but the winter sunlight was already intense, reflecting off the many mirrored surfaces punctuating the capital's skyline.

"We were talking about you," Della replied quietly. She could see his reflection in the glass; see that he looked up as she spoke the words. She turned to face him and anxiously pushed aside her fringe as it fell over her eyes. "Please don't go Gareth..."

....

Watson should have gone home, should have travelled straight back to the modern suburban house he shared with his wife and paid for by selling his soul to soulless employment. But now he wouldn't be able to pay for it, so returning there was the last thing he wanted to do. That and having to face his wife and tell her the news which would confirm her simmering suspicions that he was unreliable and not the sensible, ambitious young doctor she had hoped years ago. He wandered around the city for an hour or so, bought a chocolate muffin and then when it started to rain, found himself in a cab heading to Baker Street.

"You've been sacked," Holmes asserted at first sight of his bedraggled and careworn friend. Watson sat heavily upon the sofa thinking about whether he looked bad enough to be offered a cup of tea.

"How did you know?"

"You're here in the middle of the day when you would normally be at work, and if I'm not mistaken you've got that God-awful paperweight in your pocket which lived on the desk in your office – the one with the miniature Eiffel tower in it which you brought back from honeymoon. And you've got a stapler in your hand – why else would any sane person walk around carrying a stapler unless they had just cleared their desk? Was it the Mark Birdwhistle case?"

"Yeah, they found out what I had done. The claim got thrown out of court and the vultures, sorry lawyers, missed out on their percentage of £20,000 worth of compensation. So they threw me out. Sacked me and asked me to leave immediately. Didn't even have chance to nick any decent stationary. Oh God, my wife's going to kill me. How will I pay that massive mortgage she insisted we took out so that she could live near her sister in posh-ville?" Watson sank his head in his hands. "No book deal and now no job. Could things get any worse?"

"I've had a call from Lestrade. That Randall gang have been identified as the ones behind the Welbourne burglary last night. He wants me to go and take a look. Fancy a trip to Kent to take your mind off things? But please, don't bring the paperweight. Or the stapler."

"Lestrade called you? Oh yes, of course, Karen Welbourne's his boss. That must have felt like old times. And right now, I could really do with a bit of the old times. Ok, I'll come. A good murder is just what I need to cheer me up."

....

The last time Hopkins had seen Lestrade, he was jumping around a nightclub like a lunatic. It was quite hard for the young officer to take him seriously. But he knew better than to dismiss any input from Sherlock Holmes. And admittedly, Lestrade did cut a rather commanding figure in his expensive suit, taking Holmes around the house with the full but rather reluctant blessing of Karen Welbourne, who insisted that she just wanted to put the whole episode behind her and resist any further interference. Lestrade convinced her that it was worth letting Holmes take a look; the Randalls may have left clues or something the police could use to help track their whereabouts. Privately, he explained to his old comrade about the strange comments Karen had made to Della and that something about them had made all his old instincts stand to attention.

The Welbournes had bought the house ten years ago, a beautiful country estate perfect for a faded rock star to race around the grounds in, wearing his designer tweeds and sitting behind the wheel of a four-by-four pretending to be lord of the manor. It was a converted Abbey, named Abbey Grange at the time of purchase. The Welbournes set about adapting it to their Gothic tastes and re-named it Abbey Strange.

Watson didn't know whether to laugh or shudder at the coffins, giant crucifixes, crosses and skulls which were all part of the macabre decor. If he had come here for a little cheering up, this place was anything but cheery. And of course, there was nothing cheery about visiting the scene of a murder. But, watching Holmes do his stuff and being allowed to assist in this process was one of the things Watson found truly enjoyable in life. That and writing about it. Though he now feared that most of the accounts he had written since moving in to 221b, would never see the light of day. He felt that this wasn't just an injustice against his own talents, but even more so against the extraordinary abilities, and indeed personality, of his friend. And he knew that Holmes liked to be appreciated, even though he acted as if the opinions of others didn't matter to him at all.

DI Hopkins read the expression on Watson's face as he lifted a skull from the mantle shelf. It had diamond eyes and was covered in gold leaf.

"I know what you're thinking, strange by name and strange by nature this house. But even though it all looks a bit odd, this stuff is expensive. They spent a few hundred thou turning a perfectly decent country pile into Gothic hell," he stated, taking hold of the scull.

"Expensive," murmured Holmes, looking at the grim object with curiosity. "That's an excellent point inspector, shame you don't see its significance."

Hopkins ignored the remonstration and started to outline the case.

"Burglary is a family business for the Randalls – a father and two sons who specialise in doing over properties of the rich and famous. They did a job at Sydenham a fortnight ago – footballer's mansion while he was aboard playing in an international match. Surprised they'd do another house so soon and so nearby but they'll get life for this one – for knocking in Welbourne's head with his own poker. Its murder Mr Holmes, and anything you can give us to help locate them would be gratefully received."

"Karen Welbourne is in her bedroom Holmes," added Lestrade, "she's pretty shaken up as you can imagine but she's happy to see you."

"Then that's where we'll start," Holmes asserted.

....

Despite looking pale and shaky, it was clear that Karen Welbourne was a strong and commanding character. A handsome woman in her late fifties, her beautiful features were indicative of the fierceness and kindness which made up her formidable personality. She was sitting by the elegant sash-windows on a velvet sofa shaped like a giant pair of red lips. She looked every inch the typical rock star's wife. But there was intelligence behind her heavily made up eyes - and a deep sadness too. A well-groomed young man hovered diligently at her side, handing her a glass of water.

"Gareth, I know you are only trying to help sweetie," Karen said softly, "but I have told everything to the police and I'm not sure what else I can add for Mr Holmes' benefit."

Watson noticed that Karen's hand was shaking as she held the glass of water. She handed it back to the immaculately suited, pretty young man. "This is my PA," she added, "this is Craig Burrows." Craig smiled at the group then started to press damp cotton wool pads against a large purple swelling over Karen's right eye. She winced slightly and sat back against the sofa. "Have you been able to clear the dining room yet inspector? I just can't bare sitting here knowing that he's still down there, I understand that it's a murder investigation and these things have to be done, God knows I've watched enough episodes of CSI, but please…"

Holmes sat beside her on the lips. "The sooner I hear your account of events, the sooner I can go into the dining room and see things for myself. Please, I know it must seem tedious to have to repeat yourself but I am here to help."

For someone who was generally pretty rubbish at interacting with others, Holmes could always find exactly the right things to say, and the way to say them, when the moment required. Karen reached for the water again and as she did so, the sleeve of her black dress slipped up her arm.

"You have injuries on your arm," Holmes observed, pointing to two bright red spots.

"It's nothing" she hastily replied, pulling back down her sleeve, "not connected to last night."

After a long sip of water, she composed herself enough to begin her account.

"As you know, I am Karen Welborne. I own CEX records and manage various high-profile acts, one of which is my husband Tyler…" she paused and looked down briefly at her feet, "was my husband Tyler."

Her PA laid a comforting hand on her shoulder and she squeezed it gently before continuing with her narrative.

"There's no point trying to pretend that we had a great marriage. You only have to read the papers or talk to anyone who knew us to find out the truth. In the old days, when we were first married it wasn't so bad, but with fame came the drugs and they changed everything. Then, when my husband's star started to fade and my success continued to grow, he resented me terribly. But I'm digressing, this isn't Oprah.

Last night, my husband went to bed early due to having a heavy session with some old pals the night before. He went up about eleven. All the household staff were in bed except Craig, who sleeps in a room directly above mine. He usually stays up until I am asleep in case I need him for anything – he's so dedicated, I'm truly blessed to have him. He's worked with me for five years now.

I walked around the house to check all was ok before going to bed and ended up in the dining room. I felt a draft and noticed that the French window was open. I pulled back the curtain to close it and there was an old man standing there, frightened me to pieces. I flicked the light switch and then saw that two other men were entering behind him. I tried to step back but he caught me by the wrist, then the throat. I opened my mouth to scream but he punched me above the eye and pushed me to the ground. I think I fainted because the next thing I remember I was tied to a chair. They had cut down the bell-rope and used that to bind me, it was so tight I couldn't move and they'd stuffed material into my mouth so that I couldn't scream.

That's when Ty entered the room. I suppose he must have heard something that alerted him. He rushed at the burglars carrying a baseball bat but the old man, the first one I saw, picked up the poker from by the fire and struck him with it really hard. Tyler fell straight to the floor, didn't make a sound and didn't move. Just lay there. I fainted again; I was just so overwhelmed by what was happening. When I came-to, they had taken the silver crosses off the altar, it's just a drinks cabinet really, and had the audacity to stand there drinking a glass each of my wine.

I have already described them quite clearly to the police but I know you are going to ask me so I'll do it again. One man was elderly with a beard, he's the one who struck Ty, the other two were young, clean-shaven. They all looked to be related, father and sons. After they checked that I was still securely tied up, they left through the French window and closed it behind them.

It took me fifteen minutes of struggling to get my mouth free. Then I was able to scream for help and Craig came running into the room. That's when the police were called. Please Mr Holmes, I really don't want to go over this again.

There's nothing more I can say. I just want to be on my own, please respect that. Please."

"Of course, and thank you for being so candid." Holmes stood up from the lips and turned his attentions to Craig. "Before I see the dining room, I would very much like to hear your account of things."

Watson thought that Craig appeared nervous at this suggestion but he composed himself very quickly.

"Well it's just awful Mr Holmes," he said in a rather feminine voice. "This poor woman has endured years of ill treatment at the hands of that drugged up old has-been,"

"Craig!" Karen remonstrated.

"No Karen, I'm sorry but it has to be said. He was a piece of work and this strong, intelligent woman had to put up with his childish impossible behaviour. And now she's had to witness his death as well. It breaks my heart. I saw the men myself, three of them down by the road. I was looking out of my bedroom window and they were visible in the moonlight. I thought nothing of it at the time and shall never forgive myself for that. An hour or so later, I heard Karen scream and ran down to help her. There she was tied up, Tyler's blood on her dress. It was terrible to see her like that. Anyway, I really think you should all leave her in peace now, why should she have to keep re-living this over and over?"

He laid a protective arm on Karen's shoulder.

"I think it's time to see the dining room," Holmes said, striding from the room in his usual purposeful way when on the hunt for answers. Though Watson had to admit, this case did seem pretty clear-cut to his inferior mind. The description Karen gave fit perfectly with that of the Randall gang and the robbery was just their style, picking on the homes of the rich and famous. The way Watson saw it, this wasn't exactly a whodunit, more of a manhunt to track down the illusive gang.

As they walked through the house towards the dining room, Watson could see the irritation on Holmes' face. A gang of burglars held no particular interest to a specialist such as himself, and to be called out in response to such a commonplace, albeit unfortunate crime was frankly rather dull. Gareth Lestrade knew Holmes well enough to understand this and pulled him aside before they entered the scene of the crime. He lowered his voice as they stood in an alcove fashioned to look like a crypt.

"I know what you're thinking – there's nothing here for you, it's just a burglary gone horribly wrong. Look, I know you never held my instincts in particulary high regard, but I was a copper for over twenty years so I must have got something right. All my instincts are telling me something is wrong with this picture. I know Karen Welbourne pretty well, she's tough and feisty – this image that her and Craig are portraying of a vulnerable, fainting woman just doesn't quite ring true for me. She's trained in self defence too, I know because I recommended somewhere she could learn. The only person she's weak with is her husband – it's no secret he's been physically abusive to her. But she doesn't take crap from anyone else, that's for sure. And then there's what she said to Della yesterday. I can't help thinking it might be linked."

"Not to mention the fact that you can't actually see the road from Craig's bedroom window, not if his room is directly above hers. I couldn't see the road from her window in broad daylight, let alone moonlight."

"Please Holmes, stick around and do your thing – I feel I owe it to Karen to get to the bottom of this. She's been good to me and Della."

....

The dining room of Abbey Strange was decorated in keeping with the Welbourne's macabre tastes. The usual mix of crosses and skulls were scattered about the room, the walls were black and the ceiling a shocking pink. Giant candelabra adorned the huge black dining table and the chairs had bright pink cushions. The focal point of the room was an ornate fireplace with an oak mantelpiece. Above it was a stuffed deer's head with gold antlers and two light sabres either side. One of the dining chairs was in front of the fireplace, a thick red cord still intertwined through the back of it.

The eclectic decor wasn't enough to distract from the grim sight of Tyler Welbourne's body, lying on his back with his face turned upwards. His arms were up above his head, the baseball bat still lying in his hand. His face bore an aggressive expression and was weathered by years of hard living – or rather hard partying. His head had suffered a terrible injury and the poker which had caused it still lay beside him. It had been bent into a curve by the ferocity of the blow. Holmes examined it carefully.

"Must have been pretty strong, this old Randall," Holmes remarked, looking at the bend in the poker.

"Yeah, bit of a rough sort," replied Hopkins. "We thought the Randalls had escaped to America but obviously they couldn't resist the temptation of one more job. I am surprised though, that they'd take the risk of turning up here without their faces covered and then just leave, knowing that Mrs W would be able to give a good description of them."

"I agree. I too am surprised that they didn't silence her."

That's a first, thought Hopkins, unaccustomed as he was to Holmes ever agreeing with him.

"Maybe they didn't realise she had regained consciousness?" suggested Watson, eager to contribute something.

"He was quite a character," murmured Hopkins, ignoring Watson's efforts and looking down at the body of Tyler Welbourne. "Great showman but had a really nasty streak, especially when he'd been using. Even set fire to his wife's Chihuahua once. I don't like those pointless little dogs, but dosing one in petrol and setting it alight takes a pretty twisted mind. Then there was the time he attacked that Craig, her PA. Came at him with a baseball bat - probably the one that's in his hand now. Craig only stayed out of loyalty to Karen, wouldn't even press charges because he didn't want to make things worse for her. It was the drugs that did it. Apparently he was quite affable when not under the influence but years of snorting your millions up your nose is bound to take its toll on your mental health."

Holmes began carefully examining the knots in the rope still attached to the chair. He looked up to where the bell-rope had been cut from.

"Surely when they pulled on the rope to sever it, a bell would have rung out somewhere in the house? The kitchen maybe?"

"No, it wasn't attached to anything. Just for decoration like all the other odd things in this house," replied Hopkins.

"But the burglar wouldn't have known that."

"No, not unless he knew the house well. I've been thinking the very same thing."

"There is hope for you yet Hopkins," smiled Holmes with a curious mix of warmth and sarcasm.

"And for all this effort, they didn't take much - just the silver crosses off that alter and a few other ornaments.

Hardly worth a man's life. Perhaps they were unsettled by the murder and just wanted a quick getaway?"

"But they had time to stand around drinking a glass of wine..."

Holmes walked over to the drinks cabinet which had three glasses and a wine bottle standing on top of it.

"Have these been touched?"

"No," replied Hopkins, "all exactly as they left it."

There were three glasses standing beside each other, each with the dregs of red wine left in the bottom. One contained a few traces of cork. The bottle was beside them two thirds full. Watson noticed a change in Holmes' expression, a sudden spark of interest. He began examining the cork from the bottle.

"Probably used this to open it," Hopkins lifted a corkscrew from a draw directly in front of them.

"No, the cork was drawn using something smaller, like the screw on a pocket knife. It was driven in three times before they were able to pull the cork. Look, you can see the indentations it made. The large corkscrew would have drawn it first time. The glasses are more perplexing though, don't you think Hopkins?"

"Erm, well..."

"Karen Welbourne is certain that she saw all three men drinking?"

"Yeah, quite clear on that point. Pretty annoyed they were using her wine, almost more annoyed about that than the fact they had done in her old man."

"Well perhaps I am looking too much into things."

His keen eyes scanned around the room one last time and then Watson saw him visibly extinguish that flame of interest which had been ignited by the glasses, bottle and cork. His expression became completely passive again.

"There is nothing more I can add Hopkins. Good luck with your investigation, sounds like you have matters all sorted out in your own mind. We must return to Baker Street so that Watson can go home and take his terrible paperweight with him. Good afternoon gentleman, happy hunting."

....

Watson studied his friend's face very carefully on the train back to London. Holmes had sunk into a deep introspection, his brows drawn low and his fingertips pressed tightly together. Silence was invaluable to him in such moments and Watson respected that. He had his own thoughts to mull over anyway. His wife would be expecting him home from work soon, work he no longer had. Telling her was going to be a nightmare, especially having to tell her that it was his own fault, that he had risked his job on a point of principal. She would never understand such a thing. Not that she didn't have principals, just that she would never let them get in the way of her lovely house and comfortable life. Watson knew he was in for another night on the sofa.

Suddenly, just as the train was pulling into the next stop along from Marsham, Holmes grabbed Watson by the arm and pulled him up from his seat.

"Come on, I can't leave the case in this state. For once, I think Lestrade's instincts are right. But don't tell him I said that."

"We're getting off?"

"Yes, come on man! We need to go straight back to that dreadful house."

"Yeah, it doesn't say much about the Welbourne's sense of taste," said Watson as they bustled briskly along the aisle to the doors.

"This from the man with an Eiffel tower paperweight?" added Holmes, raising an eyebrow.

....

In a cab heading back to Abbey Strange, Watson was keen to know Holmes' thoughts. He was also thinking about how much worse his wife would react now that he was going to be late for dinner on top of sacked and hopeless.

"It's the wine glasses", Holmes suddenly said. "Let me explain, perhaps talking it through might help."

"I'm all ears," replied Watson, happy to have a distraction from his own thoughts.

"Karen Welbourne gave a very clear account of things and on the surface of it, everything she said was completely plausible and beyond suspicion. However, there are aspects of her statement which make me question its integrity. Take the Randalls for example. They stole a substantial amount from that footballer's house at Sydenham, it was a very professional, well executed job. They had no need to do another so soon and so nearby. Nor would they make the mistake of letting someone see their faces or attempting a burglary at 11pm – these things normally happen in the early hours. And if you want to stop a woman from screaming, striking her is the worst thing you can do. They hardly took anything from the Welbournes. Remember that skull we were shown with diamond eyes? How easy would it have been to grab that? Along with at least twenty other small but valuable items I noticed in the dining room. Craig lied about seeing them from his window – why would he do that? Why murder Tyler Welbourne when the Randalls could have easily overpowered him and tied him to a chair too?"

"And the wine glasses?"

"We have been told that the three men drank wine which came from the same bottle, correct?"

"Yes, they opened it and poured out three glasses."

"So, why did only one of them have bits of cork in the bottom? I checked in the bottle, the wine had many bits of cork floating around in it. All three glasses should have contained cork."

"So, what are you saying exactly?"

"That only two glasses were used and the dregs of those two were poured into a third to make it look like three people had been drinking – that's why only one glass contained all the cork. If I am correct then Karen Welbourne and her PA have both deliberately lied to us and to find the truth we must dismiss everything they told us and begin our own investigation without their help. And that's what we are about to do," Holmes said somewhat triumphantly as the cab started to pull up the long drive towards Abbey Strange.

The house was deserted except for the staff. Hopkins and his team had returned to Scotland Yard and Lestrade had persuaded Karen to stay with friends and escape the press-pack baying at the gate. The staff were surprised to see Holmes and Watson return but didn't understand what they had been doing there in the first place. They clearly weren't police, weren't press or friends of the family, and one of them had a stapler sticking out of his back pocket. But then the Welbourne entourage were so used to the family mixing with oddballs that they hardly noticed these things anymore.

When Holmes asked to be allowed to examine the dining room, nobody questioned his request and he was shown straight through. Once inside, he closed the door, an excited expression lighting up his face. He was now happily on the scent and enthusiastically set about a thorough investigation of the room. Watson sat quietly in a chair and studied his performance, watching as his friend lay upon his belly to examine the floor, dashed around looking at the rope, the windows, the chairs, the curtains, the carpet. The body had been removed but nothing else in the room had been touched or changed. Holmes found the bell-rope particularly diverting and climbed up with the help of a shelf to take a closer look. By stretching, his hand could just about reach the end of the rope where it had been cut. Suddenly, after a little cry of satisfaction, Holmes jumped down and turned his attention to the chair into which Karen Welbourne had been bound.

"Mrs Welbourne claimed she was tied into this chair when her husband was hit with the poker, correct?"

"Yeah, that's what she said."

"Right, so explain how his blood is on the seat of the chair then? Couldn't have got there if she was sitting on it. And if I'm right about the glasses, only two people were drinking – one of them at least two inches taller than me, very agile and probably carrying a pocket knife with a corkscrew attached. He knew the ways of the house and was very strong. Old man Randall looking less and less like the murderer, don't you think?"

"I don't know what to think – why would Mrs Webourne lie?"

"Well Watson that is what we must find out. This case will be perfect for your files – an excellent example of how the science of deduction can blow apart even the most plausible of statements. How foolish I was not to see the complexities of the situation straight away."

"Shame no one is ever going to read it though."

"Oh Watson for God's sake, stop feeling so bloody sorry for yourself and start using your imagination."

Watson was quite taken aback by this unexpectedly emotional outburst and didn't know how to respond – partly because he knew Holmes was right, he was turning into a bit of a whiner but didn't know what to do about it. He'd always had a tendency to wallow when things didn't go his way. It was another thing his wife found annoying about him; he wasn't 'proactive' enough.

"Alright, sorry but I did get sacked this morning Holmes, I'm not exactly having the best of days. And surely you are at least a bit disappointed that no one is going to be able to read about your unique skills? I know you didn't have a good word to say about my last book but it brought you extra business, press coverage and fan-mail. I know you liked the fan-mail Holmes, don't try to deny it. I know you keep it in a bin bag under your bed."

"Yes, I do. And even though I think your accounts lack any real methodical analysis and focus too much on the irrelevant sentimental padding you insist on throwing in, the public obviously enjoyed them. It wasn't just my fan-mail, it was yours too. All the letters include addresses. That bin bag has a couple of hundred at least. How about you stop moaning about agents and publishers, and sort out the situation yourself."

"I don't follow..."

"No you don't because you don't ever see the significance in details. Addresses Watson! Think man! Addresses of fans. Why do you need an agent and a publisher when you can access readers directly? To use an awful cliché, isn't it time to think outside the box?"

....

Watson sat on the train alone travelling back to the capital. Holmes had gone off to continue his investigations and Watson decided it was time to go home and face the music.

Holmes had planted the seed of an idea in his careworn brain – could self-publishing really be an option? As he looked out of the window watching the green fields of English countryside give way to the outskirts of London, he had to admit that it was now his only option. But what if his wife was right about him, what if he wasn't proactive enough? Surely you had to be beyond proactive to publish, sell and distribute your own book? But before he could give the idea any further serious thought, he had to go home to tell his wife that he had lost his job – a job he hated and only took to make her happy. Now, he was about to make her very unhappy indeed.

....

Gareth was surprised when he answered his mobile and heard the familiar voice of Sherlock Holmes. Holmes never called, ever. Gareth couldn't even figure out how he had got the number but he didn't mind. Holmes was a link to a past which he was now stretching away from but didn't want to forget. He was perplexed when Holmes started to question him about the Welbourne's private yacht, something which he'd had the pleasure of staying on only a few months ago. He answered all the questions without really understanding their significance and promised to look into all the other information Holmes needed. He ended the call and smiled to himself, thinking how much his life had changed in the past few years, since the days he was at Scotland Yard with a cheating wife and a career going nowhere. Now he was happier than he had ever been and knew that the best was yet to come. He had a lot to thank Watson and his book for. He decided it was time to give him a call and tell him his good news.

....

Holmes was surprised to hear the intercom buzzing at 1am. He was still up, sitting in his usual chair looking through harbour reports. Minutes later, John Watson was sitting opposite him on the sofa with a holdall at his feet. Holmes pressed together his fingertips and looked steadily at his friend, then at the bag.

"She threw you out?"

"For once Holmes, you're wrong. I walked out. I've left her. That's it, no more marriage. No more trying to please someone who I'll never really make happy. It's Lestrade's fault..." Watson paused, waiting for a response which never came. "So, go on, tell me how you know it's Lestrade's fault by the mud on my shoes or the way I've parted my hair."

Still no response. Though his level of empathy often left much to be desired, Holmes could sense his friend's pain and knew this wasn't a time for showing off his skills. He simply, calmly asked, "Why is it Lestrade's fault?" and sat back in his chair listening as Watson unburdened himself.

"Because he proposed to Della and she said yes – phoned earlier to tell me the good news. I asked him, - 'why bother?' They were living together anyway and seemed perfectly happy, and he's been down the marriage route once before and look how that turned out. And do you know what he said? He said he can't live without her and she feels the same. He sounded elated. Suddenly I thought about how well my wife and I could live without each other. How we'd both be better off. Not only is she stifling my dreams, I'm stifling hers – her dreams of a better house, the car she's always wanted, the type of husband. Do you know what I remember most about the day I got engaged? We went out with some friends on the night for a Chinese and I had a shrimp wanton for the first time – it was amazing. So the thing I always remember about that day is a shrimp wanton. Says it all really. I asked her to marry me because it seemed like the right thing to do, not because I couldn't live without her."

His eyes clouded momentarily with sadness before managing a weak, not-altogether-convincing smile – "So, I was wondering, if you're not using my old room for anything, is there any chance I could move back in?"

"There's a harpoon in there."

"I can live with that. As long as you don't try and stab me with it like you did that hat-pin once."

"That was a vital part of a murder investigation."

"It hurt!"

"There's a mannequin in there too. And a dead rat but I'm done with that now."

"Right, ok, well that's fine. I can live with that too - I suppose. Can't help out with the rent just yet as I'm now unemployed but I'll get some locum work and I can always make myself useful to you."

"You can take the mannequin back to the department store for me. I don't want them to know I'm investigating them or that I was the one who stole it. Just pretend to be one of those sex fetishists with a thing about dummies.

Confess all, cry a bit, they won't call the police. If they do I'll get Gregson to sort it out – oh actually I can't..."

"Why, what's happened to Gregson?"

"He's been sacked. Mr Kumari made a formal complaint and there was no one else to blame this time."

"Blimey. It's all change."

Silence settled between the two old friends.

"So, can I move back in?" Watson eventually asked.

"Welcome home John. Now, make yourself useful and put the kettle on."

"Some things never change," muttered Watson, with a smile.

....

Watson slept surprisingly well considering he was sharing the room with a mannequin, a harpoon and a false leg which fell out of the wardrobe at 4am and frightened him half to death. Despite all this, it was good to be back. He felt sad and rather guilty about the break-up of his marriage but knew he was right to walk away – for both their sakes. It was almost a relief now that the end had finally come. So after falling into a very deep sleep, it was a bit of a shock to be woken at 7am by Holmes impatiently prodding him in the shoulder with one of his long, bony fingers.

"Come on!" he implored, "there's work to be done Watson. Karen Welbourne has returned home and we must go there at once to unravel this little mystery she so confidently fabricated."

"Can I have breakfast first?"

"No. I've called a cab, it will be here in five minutes." And with that he bounced out of the bedroom, as eager and energetic as he always was when in pursuit of the truth. Watson rubbed his tired eyes and tried to muster the same enthusiasm whilst trying to ignore his rumbling belly.

....

Wrapped up tightly in overcoats and scarves to protect against the bitter cold of what was proving to be a very harsh British winter, Holmes and Watson rushed up the stone steps leading to the grand front door of Abbey Strange. Holmes hammered the cast-iron knocker loudly against the door and Craig the PA promptly answered.

"Ah, just the person," exclaimed Holmes, pushing past him into the spacious entrance hall. "It's time you encouraged your boss to tell me the truth, for her own sake."

"Karen Welbourne is not a liar Mr Holmes and has told you nothing but the truth. How dare you come here and say things like that."

"I know she is a wronged woman. I understand. She clearly endured years of mistreatment."

At this point, Karen herself appeared at the bottom of the stairs.

"What's going on Craig? Why are you here again Mr Holmes? I have nothing more to say to you or to anyone."

"On the contrary Mrs Welbourne, there is much to say and I urge you to say it. Please tell me your story, I come as a friend who can help. I saw the cigarette burns on your arm which you tried to hide when we first met. It is evident to me that you have been very badly treated and I will consider all of this if you would just tell me the truth."

Karen's eyes swam with tears briefly before her usual steely resolve kicked back in.

"I have told you exactly what happened Mr Holmes. Now, with respect, get out of my house."

....

Clearly frustrated that his usual persuasive manner had failed, Holmes walked so quickly away from the house that Watson struggled to keep up. He stopped suddenly beside the large pond on the front lawn. The biting cold had caused the water to freeze except for a small hole where a single swan was graciously floating. Watson caught up panting slightly and worried about how unfit a desk-job had made him. It was a blessed relief to think that he would never again have to work in no-win-no-fee hell.

Holmes watched the swan for a few moments then took out his phone. He dashed off a text and Watson noticed that the recipient was Hopkins.

"Come on," he finally said, rubbing his hands together against the cold. "Fancy a trip to the marina?"

....

Chatham Marina looked beautiful as the winter sunshine broke through the clouds. Elegant boats gleamed in its brightness and bobbed gently in the calm waters. It reminded Watson of a holiday he had taken with his wife at Brixham. They had sat on the harbour wall eating fish and chips straight from the bag. He felt a horrible pang of sadness and distracted himself by taking in his surroundings. Small rusting vessels were slotted in beside gorgeous big yachts. *Oh how the other half live* he thought to himself, wondering how some people managed to achieve that lifestyle while others chipped away at the coalface all their lives and had little to show for it. *Oh God, I'm turning into a bitter person as well as a moaning one. 'Self publish and be dammed' might be just what I need to kick myself up the ass.*

"Are you talking to me or to yourself?" Holmes asked quizzically.

"Oh sorry, did I say that out loud?"

"That's the one,"

"Sorry?"

"The Welbourne's yacht. It's over there, look – Satan's Lot. Lestrade informs me that the captain will be on board."

Watson looked up in wonder as they approached the magnificent vessel. To his surprise, it wasn't the pimped-up motorised super-yacht he was expecting. Instead Satan's Lot was a beautiful sailing yacht with magnificently polished timbers and pristine white sails stowed away while she was at rest.

"Wow, it's surprisingly tasteful," he exclaimed.

Holmes, bold as ever, unhooked the chain across the gangplank and started to walk up to the deck. Watson hesitantly followed. A terribly handsome man suddenly appeared on the deck. Mid fifties with silver hair, deep brown eyes, golden tan and physique a man half his age would envy – Captain Jack Croker was the most attractive man Watson had ever seen. He was wearing his uniform of white trousers and a fitted white t-shirt with the boat's emblem upon it – a devil's pitchfork.

"Can I help you gentleman?" he asked in a deep voice befitting his old-fashioned movie star looks. He was very tall, even taller than Holmes and not many men could claim that.

"Captain Croker I presume?" Holmes asked.

"Yes. Who am I addressing please? Are you aware that you have just come aboard a private yacht without invitation?"

"I am a friend of Karen Welbourne and act in her best interests as well as your own. Gareth Lestrade told me where to find you and this boat. The very boat you took over three months ago when the Welbournes' holidayed in Corsica. I hear that you start a new commission tomorrow. Thinking of moving on Mr Croker?"

"I can neither confirm nor deny what you speak of; confidentiality is the cornerstone of my reputation."

"And what a reputation it is Captain. I have heard not one single word against you in all of my investigations. In fact, everyone who has had dealings with you since you took the captaincy of this vessel tell of a hard working man of the highest integrity. If you would only confide in me, I will promise to take all this into consideration and urge the police to do the same. I do have some influence in that area."

Captain Croker looked around him anxiously and wrung his hands, but otherwise stayed completely calm.

"I do not know what you are talking about, nor do I wish to. Now please, I shall be speaking with the police myself if you do not leave this boat which is private property."

"I give you one more chance Captain Croker..."

"What is your name?"

"I am Sherlock Holmes and I know everything about the death of Tyler Welbourne."

There was a tense pause as the Captain studied the unyielding features of the world's only consulting detective.

"I'm sorry," he said quietly, "I can't help you. Do what you must do." Then he retreated back inside the boat and out of sight.

"With regret Watson, we must go to Scotland Yard at once. Fortunately I told the cab to wait."

....

Watson sat beside his friend in the back of the cab as it weaved through the streets finally nearing Scotland Yard. Holmes had been a silent companion on the journey and Watson's questions about Captain Croker and his significance to the investigation had gone unanswered. Holmes had slipped into a deep introspection and had a look of focused concentration upon his face. As they were on the final approach to their destination, Holmes suddenly asked the driver to pull over.

"It's no good. I've gone over and over it in my mind and can't see how any benefit can come from this course of action. Watson, do you trust my judgement? My own sense of justice?"

"Without question."

"Then let's go back to Baker Street. I need some time to think this over and you need to take back that mannequin."

"I'm not doing it – I'm not pretending to be a pervert. I know I said I'd help with your work but there are limits Holmes."

"Not for me. There are no lengths to which I will not go."

"Take it back yourself then."

"I'm happy to delegate. You look more like a pervert than me."

"Thanks. You do say the nicest things. I'm going through a midlife crisis here. I need the support and encouragement of my friends to help me through - not being told I look like a perv."

They sat in silence for the rest of the journey as the cab changed course and headed for Baker Street. Watson seriously hoped Holmes wasn't expecting him to pay half the fare.

....

Hopkins was waiting for them, standing on the doorstep huddled into his overcoat. After standing there for ten minutes he had hoped to at least be invited in, at best be given a hot drink and a few biscuits. He received neither. Instead, he stood on the doorstep and told Holmes that his text was correct and the stolen silver had been recovered from the bottom of the duck pond at the front of Abbey Strange. Clearly it had been thrown through the hole in the ice. Hopkins wanted to know why the burglars would throw away their haul.

"The burglars? So, not the Randalls anymore?"

"No Mr Holmes, they were arrested this morning in New York. They were on the other side of the Atlantic when Tyler Welbourne breathed his last. There are other gangs operating in the area so I guess we must investigate all possibilities. Do you think they were hiding the silver and intending to come back? Perhaps they were disturbed and panicked."

"Perhaps the whole thing was a blind, Hopkins."

"I just can't get to grips with it. Any hint you can give me would be gratefully received."

"I've just given you one. Now, if you are too stupid to follow it up then it's hardly my fault. I will act as I see fit. Goodnight Hopkins, it's been a long day and Watson is having a midlife crisis. We must be getting on..."

With that, he opened the door, ushered Watson inside then shut it in Hopkins' face.

"Sometimes you really are quite rude," Watson exclaimed.

"Sometimes the truth is needed. Sometimes it is best kept hidden. Hopkins is an official person and must always act on the truth. I am able to act on my own judgement."

....

John Croker turned up at 221b later that night, just as Holmes knew he would. He looked ruggedly handsome, from his stubbly square jaw to his healthy complexion glowing from the cold evening air.

"Captain Croker," said Holmes, "please take a seat by the electric fire and warm yourself. I knew you would seek me out. Who gave you the address? Was it Lestrade?"

"Yes. And he spoke very highly of your character. I have come here not for my own sake, but for Karen's and ask that if I tell you all, you will make sure I am the only one to be punished. That is my condition and you must agree to it."

"You must tell me all anyway because however stupid the Scotland Yarders are, they may work it out in the end. And they will spare no one I can assure you. My position is somewhat more flexible than theirs. Watson, please bring our visitor a drink,"

"Tea?"

"I would suggest something stronger," replied Holmes as the proud and strong figure of Captain Jack Croker visibly withered under the realisation of his situation.

Croker gratefully accepted the brandy Watson gave him.

"I regret nothing and would do the same again if I had to," he said with strong conviction. He rubbed his hand across his brow and took more brandy. "I met Karen Welbourne three months ago. The captain of their yacht was retiring and he interviewed me to be his replacement. He knew of my good reputation – I was in the navy for many years and had gone on to captain various boats belonging to the rich and famous. He told me he was happy to give me the position but that I must have a final interview with the owner. Karen took me to lunch, a lovely little cafe overlooking the sea in Ajaccio, Corsica. I thought she was the most beautiful, spirited woman I'd ever seen. I was captivated straight away. You hear of such things and think it will never happen to you, but it did, there and then at that little table with a blue chequered cloth.

I took charge of Satan's Lot and spent a blissful three weeks sailing the family around the med. Karen and I spent increasing amounts of time together as she avoided that evil brute she was married to. She was intelligent company, smart, funny and kind. Never has a man fallen so hard and so fast as I did for Karen Welbourne. Nothing actually happened between us but she was in no doubt as to my feelings. We spoke of a possible future together, I begged her to leave her unhappy marriage but she said it was hard after being Mrs Tyler Welbourne for so many years. Their lives were so intertwined that she feared losing everything she had worked for all her life. They own businesses together, a property portfolio worth millions and she's still his manager.

I had no choice other than to accept her decision but it was terrible to see the way he treated her while they were onboard – snorting drugs with his aged rock star friends then being aggressive towards her. It took all my strength and respect for her to resist throwing him overboard. Her assistant Craig was holidaying with them and I took him into my confidence. I told him about my feelings for Karen and that I'd do anything to make her happy again. He cares for her too – not in the same way as me of course but enough to understand how awful the situation is.

After their holiday ended and the Welbourne's returned to their lives, I brought the boat to Chatham and started to ask around for a new commission. I couldn't stay working for the family anymore, it was too painful. But Craig came out to see me at the marina a few times. He urged me to talk to her again, persuade her to leave Tyler and start a new life with me.

Well, I managed to secure a new position on a boat leaving for Spain tomorrow. But even though it was my intention, I couldn't bring myself to leave without saying goodbye to the woman I loved. Craig called me two nights ago, told me Tyler was in bed recovering from a heavy session and that the staff were all asleep. He said that he had left the French window in the dining room open and that Karen would go in there when she did her nightly checks. I could sneak in and speak with her without anyone knowing and causing a scandal. The staff who had been with us on the boat already suspected there was something between us. I think that even Tyler sensed there was a connection.

I live nearby in Sydenham so I raced to the house. I found the French door open just as Craig had told me it would be. As I waited in the darkness I heard Karen's voice out in the corridor. Then I heard Tyler's - they were clearly arguing. I waited silently for them to enter the room."

Croker paused in his narrative to take more brandy as the painful memories played out in his mind's eye. Looking into the amber depths of the glass he slowly continued.

"Karen turned on the light as they walked in and the argument carried on. I could see that Tyler was drunk and in a rage. I noticed to my horror that he had a baseball bat in his hand. Suddenly he lifted it and swung it at her, striking a blow just above her eye. My poor Karen cried out in pain and I rushed forward to protect her. As soon as he saw me, his rage intensified. He started swinging the bat at me, aiming for my head. I reached for the poker and struck him hard across the back of his head. I didn't realise my own strength. I was so angry with him for hurting Karen, for making the life of this brilliant, strong woman a misery. I put all of my anger into that blow and I watched as he fell to the floor. He didn't move or cry out. Karen's scream had alerted Craig and he rushed into the room.

The three of us stood there like fools simply not knowing what to do. I said that I was happy to call the police and tell them what I had done. I wasn't ashamed and had no regrets at all. That animal got what he deserved as far as I was concerned and I was happy to have freed her from his terrible ways. But Karen begged me not to make that call. She didn't want my life to be ruined because of him.

I opened a bottle of wine with the screw attached to my pen knife and urged her to take a drink to steady her nerves.

I poured myself a glass too. Craig remained calm and began to form a plan. He knew of the Randalls, as did Karen because they had recently burgled a neighbour. Their descriptions had been printed in the paper. Karen is a very intelligent woman and soon took command of the situation. I got swept along with their ideas eager to help her avoid having her own good name dragged through the mud. I jumped up and cut the bell-rope – she assured me the bell wouldn't ring as it was just for show. I tied her to a chair and frayed the end of the rope with my knife to make things look authentic. We poured the dregs from our two glasses into a third so that it would look as if three people had been drinking. She suggested some valuables I could take and they agreed to summon help fifteen minutes after I left to give me a clear run. I dropped the silver into the pond then headed quickly back to my own house at Sydenham. I lay in bed that night feeling nothing but relief that I had freed her from a monster. I intended to leave tomorrow for Spain as planned knowing that the woman I loved was safe. That is the truth Mr Holmes. Do with it what you will."

Holmes sat in silence for some time, smoking thoughtfully on a cigarette. Watson opened the window despite the cold. He had tried many times over the years to cure his friend of his smoking habit but all attempts had failed. This included patches, E-cigarettes and lists of all the shocking medical details about the damage it caused –

including photos. All this seemed to do was make him want to smoke more. So, Watson was left with damage-limitation as his only option, mainly stopping him from breaking the law and smoking in confined public places, such as on trains and once in a theatre. Holmes sensed Watson's disapproval but was clearly consumed by greater thoughts.

"I know you have told the truth Captain Croker," he finally said, "because you have told us everything I already knew. Who else other than an acrobat or a sailor could have reached the top of that rope? And it had to be someone at least two inches taller than me. The knots which secured Karen Welbourne to the chair had clearly been tied by a sailor. So all I had to do was work out when she may have come into contact with a sailor, someone with a traditional navy background who knew how to tie knots and scale rigging. And as she was shielding the person, it had to be someone she loved. Karen had made comments to Della about 'the one that got away'. This was my first clue that a lover may have some relevance to the case. When Craig lied about seeing the Randalls from his bedroom window I became convinced that the pair were covering for someone. I made enquiries with Lestrade who told me the Welbournes owned a traditional sailing yacht and had recently hired a new captain – a tall handsome man of impeccable character. The rest was easy to piece together."

"You have my respect for what you have done Mr Holmes, I only wish that I could have yours for what I have achieved in freeing the world of that dreadful man. I didn't think the police would ever work this out."

"And they haven't. Possibly they won't. I understand your motives and can see that you acted in defence of yourself and someone you care for. I'm sure that a jury would take all this into account and show leniency. But, because you have captured my sympathy, if you take that commission to Spain tomorrow, I can promise that no one will know the truth for at least twenty-four hours."

"But then all will come out?"

"For certain Croker, but by then you could be clear away."

"Well what sort of an option is that? Karen will be made an accomplice, she will be arrested. No, that's not an option at all – I cannot leave her and Craig to face the music alone for what I have done. I take full responsibility and will happily make a confession to the police as long as I can say it was all my idea and they were innocent of any wrongdoing. I don't care what happens to me."

"Congratulations," said Holmes with a smile, offering out his hand, "you've passed the test."

Croker shook his hand with a puzzled expression on his rugged features.

"I don't understand?"

"I've given the police a pretty big hint and it's hardly my fault if they are too stupid to follow it up. So, I can feel completely justified in exercising my own judgement here. You are currently our prisoner Captain Croker – I am the judge and Watson can be the jury."

"I can?" Watson asked in surprise, wafting smoke away from his face.

"I knew you and your morals would come in useful one day Watson. I can think of no better person. So, you've heard all the evidence. How do you find this man – guilty or not guilty?"

"Guilty of nothing but falling in love and wanting to…"

"Save the waffle for your books Doctor."

"Not guilty, your honour."

"And there you have it Captain Croker. You have been tried and tested in a fair manner and found innocent. I give you my word that unless another person is accused of this crime, the police will not learn of your actions from me. And I think it's unlikely they will figure it out for themselves. I suggest you take that commission and travel to Spain tomorrow then return in a year and see how things stand between you and Karen Welbourne."

Holmes opened the living room door.

"You are free to go Captain Jack Croker. I wish you well."

....

Captain Jack did indeed return to claim the hand of the woman he loved after a year at sea. By which time Lestrade had officially become Mr Della Breton and Gregson, his old rival, had followed him into security work. Only difference was that instead of landing a top job and pop-star wife, Gregson ended up as the security manager of a local supermarket, complete with cheap uniform and rather embarrassing hat.

Things had changed quite dramatically for John Watson too. Now free from 'no-win-no-fee-hell' and his dysfunctional marriage, he had taken Holmes' advice and self-published a collection of their adventures together. He proactively contacted all the people who had sent fan-mail, as well as various online groups interested in crime stories, criminology and forensic research. The response was slow at first so he learnt how to create an e-book making it easier and cheaper for people to access his work.

Gradually, word-of-mouth started to spread and the general public discovered his well-written tales about his unusual and brilliant flat-mate. Download sales grew steadily and the book started cropping up in 'top-ten' lists across the internet. Now, instead of a harpoon and a mannequin (which Holmes took back in the end – they believed his story and Watson happily remarked that he obviously looked more like a pervert than he thought - despite having cosmetic fillers in his forehead), Watson's bedroom at 221b became full of copies of his book waiting to be posted out to fans and followers. Even Defonte crawled back out from under his rock and assumed Watson would jump at the chance to be signed with him again. Instead, he politely declined – which felt so darn good.

In the end, John Watson was grateful to his midlife crisis. It forced him to examine his life and shake things up a bit. He got a new career and a very expensive watch out of it too. But most of all he was grateful to Sherlock Holmes for being annoying, arrogant, vain, brilliant and the best friend he could ever have hoped for.

Also From Charlotte Anne Walters

Barefoot on Baker Street

Whilst not always Canonical, nevertheless this is a sterling effort. The central character is unforgettable and wonderfully drawn. It's not quite as Holmes et all as some of are used to seeing him but don't let that put you off.....a worthy addition to Holmes literature. Highly recommended.

The Baker Street Society

Also From Charlotte Anne Walters

56 Sherlock Holmes Stories in 56 Days

After submitting her novel "Barefoot on Baker Street", Charlotte Anne Walters set herself the task of re-reading all the short stories in the Canon, one a day, and writing about each of them on the same day for her blog at [...]. For the book publication as "56 Sherlock Holmes Stories in 56 Days" she has added her observations on the four long stories. Her remarks are often amusing, occasionally thought-provoking and always personal and entertaining.

Roger Johnson, The Sherlock Holmes Society of London.

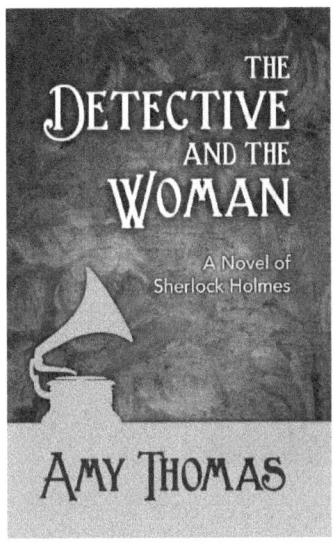 

Two acclaimed novels featuring 'The Woman', Irene Adler teaming up with Sherlock Holmes

www.mxpublishing.com

Sherlock Holmes and

The Dead Boer At Scotney Castle

In 'Sherlock Holmes and The Dead Boer at Scotney Castle' the great consulting detective comes up against the rich and powerful Kipling League. Dr Watson recounts the extraordinary events which took place on a spacious early summer day in the Sussex and Kent countryside in 1904. None of the earlier stories chronicling the adventures of Sherlock Holmes compares to the strange circumstances which determined Watson to take up his pen to relate this extraordinary adventure against Holmes' express wishes.

Links

MX Publishing are proud to support the Save Undershaw campaign – the campaign to save and restore Sir Arthur Conan Doyle's former home. Undershaw is where he brought Sherlock Holmes back to life, and should be preserved for future generations of Holmes fans.

Save Undershaw	www.saveundershaw.com
Sherlockology	www.sherlockology.com
MX Publishing	www.mxpublishing.com

You can read more about Sir Arthur Conan Doyle and Undershaw in Alistair Duncan's book (share of royalties to the Undershaw Preservation Trust) – *An Entirely New Country* and in the amazing compilation *Sherlock's Home – The Empty House* (all royalties to the Trust).